Blink Once

Blink Once

CYLIN BUSBY

BLOOMSBURY

NEW YORK LONDON NEW DELHI SYDNEY

First published in the United States of America in September 2012
by Bloomsbury Books for Young Readers
www.bloomsburyteens.com

For information about permission to reproduce selections from this book, write to
Permissions, Bloomsbury BFYR, 175 Fifth Avenue, New York, New York 10010

Library of Congress Cataloging-in-Publication Data
Busby, Cylin.
Blink once / by Cylin Busby. — 1st U.S. ed.
        p.   cm.
Summary: West, a high school senior with everything going for him until an accident leaves him
paralyzed, connects with Olivia, a patient in the hospital room next to his, who seems to
understand his dreams and nightmares but who has a secret.
ISBN 978-1-59990-818-2 (hardcover)
[1. Paralysis—Fiction.   2. People with disabilities—Fiction.   3. Hospitals—Fiction.   4. Haunted
places—Fiction.   5. Nightmares—Fiction.   6. Love—Fiction.]   I. Title.
        PZ7.B9556Bli 2012   [Fic]—dc23   2012011232

Book design by Nicole Gastonguay
Typeset by Westchester Book Composition
Printed in the U.S.A. by Quad/Graphics, Fairfield, Pennsylvania
2 4 6 8 10 9 7 5 3 1

For Dad, who has been there and back

All that we see or seem
Is but a dream within a dream.
                    —EDGAR ALLAN POE

Blink Once

Chapter 1

Someone is crying. A girl. Not a pretty kind of crying, like actresses do, tears delicately streaming down a beautiful face. This is sobbing, sniffling, gasping for air. Crying hard. I have to wake up. I have to help her, whoever she is. I force my eyes open, but I don't see anyone. I see a white wall with a machine attached to it. I make out a blood-pressure cuff and a large dial, like in a doctor's office. The crying suddenly stops. Where is she, the crying girl? I have to find her. Something is wrong, really wrong. I try to sit up, get out of bed, but I can't. My arms are strapped down. My legs are trapped somehow; I'm flat on a bed and I can't move. I can't speak. I can't move my head, can't move my mouth. My heart is racing. I'm falling, I'm falling.

———

My throat was killing me. So dry, raw, I couldn't swallow. Like the worst sore throat ever. I opened my eyes. Was it a school day? What time was it? What day was it? I felt like I was lying at a strange angle—I was on my stomach, but I could see the floor below me. It seemed I was hovering, floating there. And I couldn't move. I saw the tile floor under me; it was green and white. *I'm falling*, I thought. *But I'm not falling. I'm hanging.*

I blacked out.

When I woke up again, I was looking at white tiles—ceiling tiles this time. I knew one thing: I was in a hospital. My throat hurt so bad, the pain was deafening. I couldn't think about anything except for how badly it hurt. Then I heard a sound; it was my own voice going "Ahhhhhhhhh."

Around me, it was quiet. I could hear some kind of machine running—pumping, swooshing air right next to my head. There was a beeping sound on the other side, very steady. *Beep.* Pause. *Beep.* Pause. *Beep.*

I was able to look around a little bit but not much. Something circled around my head, my shoulders, something big and white; I could see it if I moved my eyes all the way to the right or left, but I couldn't actually turn my head. "Ahhhhhhhhhhh," I kept saying. I tried to say, "Thirsty." But I was so dry, the words didn't work. Something was up my nose. I tried to touch my hand to my face and feel what was there. But my hand couldn't move; there was something across my wrist, holding it down. I couldn't see it by looking down. My other wrist too. What was going on? Who did this to me? *Why?*

———

There was a woman next to the bed when I woke up again. She was holding my arm at the wrist and staring at a machine. I was able to look down and see my arm in her hands. It looked okay, not swollen or anything, just my regular arm. But it felt funny, like it was covered in a layer of blubber. "Ahhhhhhhh," I said to her. She looked over at me and smiled. I felt my muscles relax. Thank God, an actual person to tell me what was going on.

"How are you doing, Mr. West?" she asked me, but then looked away like it was no big deal that I was awake. Had I been here long? Where were my parents? "Ahhhhhhhhh," I tried again.

"Okay." The nurse patted my arm. "You're okay." I saw her put my hand down and rub the back of it, then she slid my arm under something that looked like a wide belt across the bed. It felt weird, like she was wearing a thick glove. She snapped something metal down by my feet and did the same thing above my head. "Here we go," she said softly, then somehow the bed turned and I was suddenly lying sideways, at a ninety-degree angle. I must have been strapped in or I would have fallen right onto the floor. But I didn't. I just lay there rigid, strapped to the bed, looking at a wall and a doorway. And that's when I met Olivia.

I didn't really meet her; I heard her. That's not right either—I heard her mother.

After rolling me sideways, the nurse left without even asking me if I wanted some water. I heard shoes, high-heeled shoes clicking on the tile floor, and saw a woman pass the doorway. She was tall and thin and wearing something red, a suit or a long jacket or something. She walked past my doorway, into the room next door to mine. There wasn't a real wall between the rooms, just one of those big, thick accordion-screen things. It was all the way closed, but I could still hear almost everything. "Hello, darling!" a voice said brightly. I assumed it was the woman in red.

"I've brought you your favorite flowers, pink roses. See how tiny they are? They're called miniature roses. I thought you'd like these." I liked listening to her voice. She sounded foreign, like she was French or Italian or something. I heard her pull a chair across the floor. "Let me tell you about my day. I wish you could have been with me. I went to Nordstrom's and I tried on so many bathing suits. *C'était terrible.*"

I waited to hear a response from the person she was talking to, but she said nothing, just listened to this woman's boring shopping story. Then I started thinking about bathing suits. Wait. It was winter. Why would someone be shopping for a bathing suit in the winter? I felt hot all over, sweat on my face like I was having a panic attack. What month was it? Then the woman mentioned a trip she was going on with some man and how happy she would be to get away from this "snow and dreadful weather" and how she wished she could take her "little angel" with her. I was so happy to hear that it was still winter.

Her voice got softer and softer as she went on, so soothing, I could tell she loved the person she was talking to. I realized she was saying everything I wanted to hear: that it was all going to be okay, that she was here now. My eyes closed for a second, and when I opened them again, I was still staring at the same wall.

Over the sound of the machines around me, I listened for the French lady. I could hear someone humming. I tried to speak, but just ended up making that sound again.

"So, you're awake," a voice floated over to me from somewhere I couldn't see, somewhere behind me. "I'm your neighbor, Olivia. I already know your name is West. Don't bother trying to talk. You have a respirator tube in."

The second she said it, the feeling in my throat made sense: a tube. That whooshing machine: a ventilator. What did that mean, how bad off was I? I heard the sound of something being rolled and then there was a girl in front of me. A small girl with huge dark eyes. "And by the way, you're paralyzed, in case no one's told you yet."

No. That couldn't be right. I was not paralyzed. I could move. I tried to wiggle my hands, but my wrists were strapped down. I wasn't paralyzed, just strapped in. I tried to lift my fingers to show her, but I couldn't be sure they were moving.

"Don't believe me?" she asked. She moved to my bed, pulling her IV stand along beside her. There were tubes going into her arm and the back of her hand. I saw her reach out one arm. "Feel that?" she said, standing at the foot of the bed. "Of course you don't—you're paralyzed, that's why."

I tried to check in with my lower body. I could feel it, I could feel the weight of my legs attached to me. They were there. I tried to move my foot. Did it move? I couldn't tell; it felt like my legs were strapped down too, like they were wrapped up in something thick. But if I could feel that, didn't that mean something? I felt my heart start to beat fast again, that awful sweaty, cold feeling sweeping through me. This girl was wrong. Why would she come in here and start telling me this horrible stuff like it was no big deal?

Olivia rolled her IV stand to the chair in the corner and gathered her white robe around her tiny body as she sat. "Sorry if you didn't already know. I'm sure you're bummed. I'm a dancer, so if that happened to me, if I were paralyzed, I would just . . . I don't know what I would do," she said quietly.

I'm not paralyzed! I wanted to yell at her. Get out, just get out. Until my parents can get here and explain to me what is going on, I don't want to hear what you have to say.

She looked down at her feet and pointed and flexed them a few times. "I bet you're wondering why I'm here," she said, pushing her dark bangs from her eyes. "I used to weigh about eighty-five pounds, but I'm sure I look so different now, you'd never know. It's from lying in a bed all day, and this"—she pointed to her IV bag on the metal pole—"that's liquid nutrition. So tasty!" She smiled, and I noticed her teeth were tiny, like a child's, and a funny color, like a dark white, but maybe that's because her skin was so white her teeth looked strange next to it.

I knew girls like her. Crazy eating-disorder chicks. She was probably going to sit in here all day and tell me about every calorie she ate.

"You were on a mountain bike when you had an accident; I heard your parents talking about it." She watched my face. "Do you remember?" She stared hard at my face, like I could answer. "Just blink once for yes and twice for no," she sighed, exasperated.

I blinked once, then blinked twice fast. Was I blinking? It felt like I was; maybe my face was paralyzed too. I felt like I couldn't move my lips.

"You do remember it, or not?" Her eyes were like black marbles, no pupil. They were pretty but in a scary way, with her pale skin and dark hair. I blinked twice this time, just to answer her, but really I was confused. I couldn't totally feel my legs and my arms felt so funny.

I tried hard to remember what the last thing was before . . . here. It was foggy, like a dream the morning after you sleep too much. I remembered Allie, my girlfriend. Her blond hair blowing in her eyes, she's watching me. I'm at the dirt-bike trail by the quarry in the woods with Mike; we're doing jumps. And . . . and then, what happened next? I had only fragments. Suddenly I did remember. Something bad had happened. Someone got hurt. Someone was crying.

Olivia's voice cut through my thoughts. "I didn't think you'd remember it, not yet," she said. "It'll probably come back to you later," she added quietly. "That's how it was for me, too." I wanted her to stop talking for a second so I could think. But my thoughts were all scrambled. I couldn't focus on one thing for more than a few seconds. My throat was killing me.

Olivia watched me; her face looked sad for a second, then she stood up and pulled her IV stand behind her. "It's almost six. That means your mom will be here soon—she always comes around then." She pulled her baggy robe around her and left without saying anything, even good-bye.

———

"There's my boy." At the sound of Mom's voice, I woke up. Had I been sleeping? Was it still the same day—wasn't that girl just here? My mom. I wanted to see her so badly.

"Hi, hon." Mom came around the bed to where I could see her, and it was her. She was acting so normal, looking so normal in her same old clothes, her long navy-blue wool coat, it was like she had just come home and found me sitting on the couch watching TV. She pulled over the chair and sat right beside me, pushing my hair out of my face. "I know you'll hate me for saying this, but I think we need to do something about this hair. It's just going to drive you crazy."

Her face was calm; she was smiling a little bit, looking me right in the eye. Why was everyone acting so normal? Didn't they all get it—I was lost, I felt like I had amnesia or something. I tried to speak. "That tube is still bothering you, isn't it?" She wiped the corner of my eyes. "I'm so sorry, I wish I could take it out but you need it in there to breathe, okay?" My hair fell across my eyes again and she pushed it back, stroking my forehead. "I'm so lucky to have you, you know that? You're getting so much stronger every day, and pretty soon you'll be able to go home, pretty soon."

I made the only sound I could, a grunt, like a throat clearing. I saw my mom look up at the doorway. "That tube is giving him a hard time again—can you check it, please?" she said to someone behind her.

"Sure, Mrs. Spencer. It's time to rotate his mattress

again," said a female voice. It sounded like the nurse from before, the one who checked my blood pressure, and as she came into view, I saw that it was her—an older, round woman in a nursing uniform with her hair pulled back from her face. She loosened something at the foot of the bed and then pulled the mattress back to flat, so I was lying on my back, staring at the ceiling. "He'll need some eye drops, too." The nurse held a tiny flashlight over my eyes for a second, making me squint. "You're sure you don't want us to tape his lids shut? It can help keep irritation down," the nurse added, looking at my mom.

"Oh no, he'd hate that, please don't," Mom told her.

The nurse shrugged. "Your call." She picked up something from a tray next to the bed and then dropped some liquid into my eyes that made my vision go all blurry and my eyes feel greasy. I felt the nurse touching my neck, my throat. She was tugging on something. "Do you mind if I flush this out while you're here?" she asked my mom. "It can be a little messy."

"Actually I have to leave early today, so I'll just say good-bye and let you get to work," she said. She leaned over me where I could see her face. "Sorry I can't stay too long today. Bye, sweetie. I'll see you tomorrow, okay?" She kissed my cheek and gave me a smile. She never even took off her coat.

The nurse waved to her as she left. "Your mom is a

good lady," she said softly, leaning over me as she worked on the tube in my throat. "Not everyone is so lucky." The nurse motioned with her head to the wall that separated my room from Olivia's. "That one's mother is a real piece of work," she whispered, shaking her head. "Nothing's ever good enough for her Olivia. Piece of work," she said again, pulling up a clear plastic tube. "No wonder this is bothering you. Let's see that chart," she said, walking to the foot of my bed where I couldn't see her. She was still talking, but now it was quietly, and mostly to herself. "Have to remember to talk to Cheryl. . . . Thinks you can't feel it. . . ." I could hear her writing something on the chart, scratching the paper with a pen.

Then she was back over me, her tight face bunched up as she worked on my throat. Her dark-brown eyes were focused on my neck. I felt cool water suddenly inside my throat. I tried to swallow, but it felt like it was too low to swallow so it just went down on its own. "Good job," the nurse said, pushing something into my throat. "That's better now, huh?" she asked me.

It did feel a lot better and I wanted to tell her, so I blinked once for yes. I hope she got the message. Was that what Olivia said, once for yes, twice for no? Or was it twice for yes? The nurse took my hand and held it at the wrist while looking at her watch for a few seconds. "Okay, doing great." She tucked my hand and arm back under the belt on the bed. "Get some rest now." She winked at me and left the room. I stared at the ceiling, trying to soak in everything that was going on—or not going on—and listening to the noise of the machines next to my bed.

This can't be happening, this is a dream. A bad dream. I closed my eyes and tried to get myself to wake up. Wake up in my own bed, putting this behind me. I had learned my lesson. I would be more careful on the bike. I would not show off for Mike or anyone else. I could make this all go away. *This isn't real. This isn't real. This isn't real.*

Chapter 2

The winter sun is setting and the glare keeps getting in my eyes. I pull down the visor on my helmet and wipe my gloves on my jeans. "Let's do this!" I hear Mike yell as he zooms by me, his legs pumping the pedals. He's standing up on his bike and hits the wooden ramp going fast, almost too fast. He slides smoothly up the incline, yanking his bike to the right and his body to the left, jumping back on his wheel jacks hard and bouncing the tire up to the ramp ledge. "Whooooooooooo!" he yells, pulling his bike up on its rear wheel beside him, like a trophy fish. "Come on, hit it!"

With the sun behind him, he looks like a photo negative, a black cutout against the red and orange sky. I flip up my visor and turn to look at Allie. She's sitting on that big rock, watching us, but I know she must get bored with all this. She tilts her head and looks back at me, that little smile on her face. I snap the visor back down and wheel around, get far enough from the ramp to get some distance, some speed, some air.

I'm moving fast, standing on the pedals and pushing hard. I love it when the bike just feels like another part of me, an extra limb, connected. I hit the ramp but something's wrong. The wheel pulls to the right so I pull left—too hard. I'm gonna spill, maybe even backward. I feel it coming, that loss of control, that idiot feeling. Damn, I hate giving Mike something to talk smack about. I yank my arms up to break my fall, but they won't move. They're stuck, strapped down. I keep pulling them up, but I can't . . . I can't . . .

———

And then I woke up, straining against the strap across my bed. I was still here, it was real. I was in a hospital, paralyzed, or at least that's what the girl next door said.

"Hey there, mister, calm down, you're okay," the nurse said. "Where do you think you're going?" She pulled my arm out from under the strap and held my wrist. "Heart's racing; what kind of dream you having?" She was looking me right in the eye, as if I could answer her. I didn't even know how long I'd been here, but for the past two days I'd seen this same nurse. She talked to me like she knew me, but maybe all the nurses did that.

She wiped my forehead with a small towel. "Getting your exercise in your sleep, huh? Wish I could do that," she said. "Instead, they got me counting my points and walking on that treadmill every day. Huh!" She smiled at me. "Now how many points do you think there are in a chicken salad sandwich? Well, you'd be surprised. A whole lot, that's how many." She clicked the mattress at the top, then at the bottom, and rotated the bed ninety degrees. "There, now you can look outside." Beyond her was a big window, winter sun streaming in.

"You have a good day now," the nurse said, and left the room. At least I think she left; they all wore such quiet shoes, it was hard to tell.

I must have drifted off again, because the next thing I heard was someone talking. "You awake?" a voice said. Olivia. The room was getting dark now, dusk settling in.

She sniffled and rolled her IV pole around the bed so I could see her. There was no chair on that side, so she just sat on the other bed that was there, pulling her knees up to her chest. She looked like she'd been crying.

"Oh, thank God you're awake," she said, looking at my eyes. She was quiet for a moment, just looking down. "Do you know how long I've been here?" After waiting a beat or two for my answer, she laughed. "I'm so desperate, I'm having a conversation with a human vegetable!" I blinked twice. I'm not a vegetable.

"Okay, you're not a vegetable," she said, as if she could hear my thoughts. She lay on her side, tucking her robe carefully around her skinny legs. Her modesty made me sad—like I would really try to sneak a look up her hospital gown.

"I'm just so tired of being treated like a child, you know?"

I blinked yes.

"This is not what we're supposed to be doing at sixteen. We're supposed to be having fun."

I blinked twice, no—also because I wasn't sixteen; I had just turned seventeen.

"Let's do something," she said slowly. "No TV until free period tonight. You obviously are not up for a game of checkers, are you?" She grinned. "I mean, we could try it—I could move your pieces based on yes-or-no blinks, but . . . I think maybe not." Her sense of humor was growing on me. Maybe she wasn't so bad. "I'll read to you. You like it when your mom does that." I didn't remember my mom reading to me. How could Olivia know about it when I didn't? Had I been unconscious that long?

She opened the bedside table and took a book out of the drawer. *Harry Potter and the Sorcerer's Stone*. It looked like my copy of the book. But I hadn't read that in years—it was so like my mom to bring in that book. She was always pulling out stuff from when I was little and trying to make it relevant now, like she didn't want to let go of me at age ten or twelve or something. When Olivia opened the book and started reading, I was surprised by how quickly I slipped into the story and forgot about what was going on. I liked her voice and her pale white face, her lips so red as she formed the words.

When I discovered Harry Potter, I ripped through the books at lightning speed. I was ten and I guess I was what you would call a nerd. Actually, I had no idea how nerdy I was until I met Mike. Mike was the person who saved me from a high school career of being a complete outsider. I had to give him total credit: he sought me out, made friends with me. Of course, he did it for totally selfish reasons— he wanted someone to bike with. But I was saved from nerdom, and got a best friend in the bargain, so I'm not about to complain.

I'm not sure if Mike and I ever talked about Harry Potter. If he knew that, at one time, I was obsessed with those books. It's not the kind of thing he and I would ever talk about—books, reading. It only took Olivia about twenty-four hours to figure it out, and I've never actually spoken a word to the girl. As I watched her mouth move, I couldn't help noticing her face was really pretty, and I was hardly hearing the words. Before I knew it, I was asleep again.

When I woke, it was dark and I was facing the floor. I'd been rotated again. I didn't know how much time had passed, or even whether it was the same day. But something woke me up. Someone was crying—Olivia, in her room?—but it was closer than that, and I could see, looking to the side, that the door to my room was now shut. Who was crying? It felt like a dream, like a dream I had had before.

That's when I saw feet, beside my bed, by the small table. They were not in nurse's shoes, but in sandals. Painted toenails. Little girl's feet. She was sniffling and doing something in the drawer by my bed, pulling things out of it. Who was this person? She pushed the drawer shut and walked away, still sobbing, sniffling, but her sounds growing more distant as she left the room. I didn't hear the door close behind her.

I tried to clear my throat, but I knew the sound wouldn't be loud enough for Olivia or the nurses to hear. The next thing I knew, it was bright in the room, and the nurse was rotating my bed. I must have fallen asleep again.

"I heard from your mom today," the nurse told me, dropping some liquid into my eyes. "She's not going to be able to make it after work tonight and she wanted me to let you know. I told her that you wouldn't be any trouble at all, so don't make me out to be wrong, okay?" She smiled, and I noticed that she had a big space between her front teeth. Something about that made me instantly like her even more than I already did.

"All right, handsome, you have yourself a good day,"

she said, hanging my chart on the foot of the bed and leaving the room.

I couldn't really wake up. With all the sleep I was getting, you would think it would be easy to be awake, but I drifted in and out, unable to tell what time it was or what day. Sometimes a nurse went down the hall. Another time, someone in a lab jacket came into my room and looked at my chart. Maybe they were giving me some painkillers that were fogging my mind; something was going on, and I couldn't seem to even focus. How long had I been here anyhow? Suddenly, someone leaned over me.

"Boo!" Olivia said. She was holding her IV pole beside her, and pulled over a chair. "More *Potter* this evening, I presume?" From the light, I could tell that it was evening already—another day had passed in a blur with no visitors, not any that I knew of, and no doctor to tell me what was going on.

I blinked once for yes.

"Really, I was thinking of something a little racier, like *The Scarlet Letter*, but if you want *Potter*," she joked, opening the drawer. I thought about my dream—or had it been?—from the night before. A girl opening the drawer. Who had that been, in my room?

Olivia read a chapter, one that I actually remembered pretty well, and I was proud to stay awake through the whole thing. When she looked down at my face, I knew she was checking to see if I was still awake, so I blinked once. Yes, I'm still here.

"You're doing better," she said, her eyes opening wider. "I can tell. That's good." She got quiet for a second and just looked out the window at the dark. "I need a friend," she finally said, very matter-of-fact. "I know that sounds weird, but . . . I just don't have anyone to talk to. And . . . I probably shouldn't even tell you this," Olivia started to say. Then she met my eyes and smiled. "But if I don't tell you, who will I tell?"

She closed the book and set it on her lap, holding it in both hands. After a deep breath she said, "There was a guy in this room before you . . . before you came here. He was very sick, I don't know what was wrong with him. No, that's not true." She stopped herself and met my eyes. "I do know, or I think I know. But that's not the point. He was here for a while, but he was in a coma or something. At first he had a lot of visitors; I watched them come and go, you know, the same way I do with you sometimes. Not spying, just bored." She smiled and pushed her hair back. "But then, something happened: the visitors came less, even the doctors came less." She shook her head. "By the time I really noticed, it had been weeks since anyone had come to see him. I started watching more closely during visiting hours, just to be sure. But no one came. And the weeks stretched into months. It made me really sad. But then, as time went by, it made me really angry." Olivia swallowed. "Then one day, he was gone. Just like that. We woke up one morning and he was . . . the room was just *empty*."

She looked up at me and her eyes were watery. "Look, I'm not an idiot. I know this is a place where they stick kids that no one cares about. It's a place where they send kids who everyone has given up on. But . . ."

Was Olivia trying to say that this was going to happen to me? That no one cared about me? That wasn't true. But then a cold feeling went through me. I thought about my mom's visit, how she stayed for just a few minutes. She didn't even take off her coat. Then tonight, she couldn't come at all.

Olivia went on. "Something's just not right about the whole thing. Sometimes at night, I get a funny feeling— about him. And I mean, this was his room." Olivia hugged the book to her chest and scanned the darkening corners. "Have you ever . . ." She caught herself again. "I know this sounds so creepy and morbid, but have you ever seen or heard anything . . . weird in here?"

I had to think hard. My reality had been blurry since I woke up here. Drifting in and out of consciousness, the weird dreams, not knowing what was real and what wasn't. And then there was Olivia and how I felt about her. Half terrified and half captivated. I was in over my head in so many ways; how could I judge what was weird and what wasn't?

I blinked once. Then just as a smile crept across

Olivia's face, I blinked twice. Maybe there was something. A dream I had. Or was it real? That girl. Someone crying.

"Is that a yes, no, or maybe?" she asked, and seeing me blink twice, added, "Sort of?" She leaned in close to me.

I blinked yes.

"Was it something you saw? A feeling? A dream?" she whispered.

Yes.

Her face was so close to mine, I could smell her clean scent. I felt my heart skip a beat. I was wide awake now. She held my eyes for a moment longer than she needed to. Then, suddenly, she sat back and put the book into the drawer.

"It's probably nothing. I mean, don't be scared to sleep in here tonight or anything. You won't be, right?" she asked casually, like she was embarrassed by what had just happened between us. *Did* something happen between us?

She glanced at the clock. "They'll be around soon with night meds, so I'd better scoot." It sounded like she was forcing herself to be light, like everything was okay. She went to the accordion wall and slid it open, sneaking through the crack. "Night," she tossed over her shoulder, pulling the wall shut behind her. So that's how she was able to get in without the nurses or anyone else seeing her.

I realized all at once that, just like I could hear her mom and nurses talking to her, she could hear everything going on in my room. She must have heard everything that went on with the guy in this room before me: every visitor, every doctor, and every nurse. No wonder it freaked her out when . . . when whatever happened happened. But my situation wasn't anything like that. I wasn't in a coma. I wasn't even really paralyzed. That wasn't going to happen to me, so she was worried for no reason. At least that's what I told myself as I started to drift off. I wouldn't think about the guy who was in here before me, and what happened to him. I was going to get better and get out of here. Hang out with Allie and Mike, and go to school and be regular again. I was going to do it. No way that was going to happen to me. No way.

Chapter 3

I'm walking. It's dusk. It's a sidewalk I've never been on before. But I know this part of town. There's a famous theater here, where they do *The Nutcracker* every Christmas, and a dance studio next door. I look up at the windows, all lit up, a wooden bar running along one wall and mirrors everywhere. Girls doing ballet moves are lined up along one wall. Long bare legs, pink leotards. I watch them for a second, then I look away embarrassed, like I've been caught doing something dirty, and stare down at my boots as I walk. When I look up again, I don't know where I am; I'm lost. The street is no longer the same. I turn, but the theater is gone. There's a burned-down building instead. I'm scared; something's not right. I want to run. I hear someone in the bushes next to me; when I look, I see a couple. I can just see his back.

She's saying GET OFF ME and he's hissing something at her, swearing, saying horrible, sick things. I want to help her, but I look down and see that my legs are tied together, I can't move. My arms are tied down. I'm all tied up and suddenly, this guy—he's standing in front of me.

"You're okay," he says. "It's okay now"—but his voice is ragged and mean. He reaches out to touch my cheek and I see blood on his hand, his knuckles are raw and red like he's been in a fight, like he's been punching someone hard. *Don't touch me, don't touch me, don't touch me*, I'm screaming, but it's like I'm underwater, I can't even hear myself. His bloody hand touches my face, I feel a rough finger on my cheek.

———

"You're okay, it's okay now." The nurse had her hand on my forehead. It was the same nurse I'd seen before, the super-nice one. "You're gonna be just fine. Me, I'm not so sure." She smiled, motioning to her uniform. "This is courtesy of you and your heart-rate monitor going off." There was a light brown stain down the front of her white top and along one leg. "I was all ready to have myself a nice cup of tea and a couple of cookies." She used a syringe to put something into my IV and I felt it cold in my veins. "There, that's gonna help you calm down and rest, no more bad dreams."

She dropped something that clanged on the floor, glass or metal, and it echoed into the empty, dark hallway beyond my room. "Sorry about that, I'm still shaking. This place is so quiet at night." She wiped a cool cloth over my forehead and looked into my eyes. "When one of these monitors goes off at the station, I just about pee my pants!" She laughed and took a small flashlight from her pocket. She quickly flashed it into my right eye, then the other one. "Okay, heart rate looks good. Now, young man, don't scare me any more tonight. I can't take it." She patted my hand and let out a sigh. "Good night, handsome," she said, and leaned over the bed to tuck me in. "Sweet dreams now." As she left the room, she switched out only one set of lights, leaving the other set on, which I was grateful for, and she closed the door only halfway.

When she stepped outside my door, I heard her gasp. "Oh my Lord, you all are determined to give me a heart attack tonight! I was not expecting to see you at this hour!" Her voice trailed off as she led the person away from my door. But I knew who it was: Olivia. She probably heard the heart monitor and got freaked out. The nurse would tell her I was okay, but now I would have to face her questions tomorrow. I tried to look at the clock, but the numbers and lines all floated around together, making no sense. Whatever she gave me was strong and worked fast.

I didn't want to think about the dream, or slip back into it, like I sometimes do, so I tried to think of something else. I thought about Mom visiting me, and maybe seeing

Allie. When was I going to see her again? How long had it been since I had seen her? I thought about the way her hair smelled like her shampoo, like flowers.

When she broke up with me last year, I went into a drugstore one day and actually went to the shampoo aisle to look for it. I couldn't remember what it was called, so I kept opening bottles and sniffing them, like a total freak, until a clerk who worked there told me I wasn't allowed to open a bottle unless I was going to buy it. I bought two bottles of random shampoo just so I wouldn't look like a weirdo pervert who got off on sniffing shampoo. I never told Allie about that.

As I was drifting off, I thought I saw a figure standing by my bed, a shadow. For an instant, I thought it was him, from the dream, and I really was tied down, powerless. Then I blinked and I could see that it was just Olivia. She must have waited for the nurse to go back to her station and snuck out again, coming in through the room divider this time.

"You okay?" she whispered. She looked different; it took me a second with my foggy brain to figure out why. Her hair was down, long and dark around her face. It looked good. She touched my hand, and I felt her warmth as her fingers traveled up my arm to rest on my shoulder, then higher, to my face. I blinked and she smiled, her face so close to mine. "I was worried but you're okay now, right? I'll stay with you."

Her hand on my face felt amazing, so different from the hand in my dream. Soft, warm, small. No one but the nurses had touched me in so long. How long had it been? I wanted her hand to stay on me forever. She stroked my cheek and I couldn't even tell her how good it felt, that I wanted her to never stop.

———

When I opened my eyes, Olivia was still there, sitting by the bed. "You just missed your mom." She looked up from her book and gave me a look like she was pissed at me. What happened to the sweet whispering girl from last night?

"What did they give you? You were loopy." I noticed she had changed out of her pajamas and had her hair in a ponytail again, so she hadn't been with me all night. I liked her hair down better, but she still looked good. It kind of bugged me that she was beautiful, probably because I was meeting her when I was like this. I didn't stand a chance.

"While you were playing the lead role in *Sleeping Beauty*, I had this idea," Olivia went on, and from the smirk on her face, I was a little concerned. "You know, when we were trying to talk last night, it was really hard to um, communicate? And then I know you had a bad dream—wait, was it about the room? Oh my God, did you see a ghost or something?" I blinked no and she was noticeably disappointed.

"Well, I'm sorry if talking to you before bed made you have a bad dream or something," she said dismissively, like she wasn't really sorry at all.

"Look." She brought out a small whiteboard. "It's a wipe-off board, you know?"

I blinked yes.

"And I was thinking . . ." She looked from the corner of her eye to the doorway and put her hands on the straps over my right wrist. "Let's just see . . ." She undid the straps, never taking her eye off the door. "I think we have about half an hour before your next check."

She put a thick black marker into my hand and closed my fingers around it. It instantly dropped onto the floor. Olivia let out a grunt. "Well, you have to hold it," she scolded. She put it into my hand and closed my fingers around it again, squeezing tight. "Can you hold it?" The way she said it was more like a taunt than a question.

I sent a message to my hand to close on the pen, but it was hard to feel whether I had it in my fingers—they felt like giant sausages, with layers of something wrapped around them. I squeezed as tight as I could and hoped for the best.

"YES!" Olivia cheered, then looked to the doorway. "I mean *yes*," she whispered more quietly. "You've got it." She held the board next to my hand where I could see it if I turned my head to the side a little. "Okay . . . go for it."

Suddenly, the room got very quiet. I heard her breathing, and the sound of the respirator, the blips of the machines attached to me. I tried to cut everything else out and just focus on moving my hand the way I wanted to. It jerked right, cutting a thick black mark across the board. Olivia moved my hand back into place and positioned the board.

"Try again," she said sternly. "I know you can do this."

I moved my hand a little less this time, making a smaller black mark—not exactly a line, but a smear. I dropped my hand a little lower and made another. Two lines next to each other. I made a third line. Olivia broke into a huge smile. "You're doing it!"

She turned the board around to look at it and nodded. I jerked the pen. "You're not done?" she asked, and I blinked no. She put the board back next to my pen and I slowly finished what I wanted to do: a line slashed across two of the lines, making a sideways *H* and a blobby mark over the third line. Done.

Olivia turned the board around. I could tell she was trying to figure out what I wrote. "Hi," she read. She closed her eyes for a second, and when she opened them, I saw that watery look again. "Hi to you too," she finally said. She rubbed her hand over her face and took a deep breath. "Well, this changes everything, huh, stranger?"

Footsteps outside my door sent her scrambling. "Oh crap, I'm gonna get in so much trouble with Norris!" She grabbed the pen from my hand and quickly attached my straps so clumsily, the nurses were sure to notice. "I was not here, got it?" She tucked the board under her arm and scooted quickly from the room, closing the wall behind her.

Chapter 4

The footsteps we heard in the hall didn't belong to Nurse Norris. I should have known—in their soft shoes, you never heard the nurses coming.

In the doorway, I saw a flash of bright blue, a mass of curly blond hair.

It was Allie.

She looked so good, her cheeks rosy from the cold. She was wearing her winter coat, the puffy ski jacket that matched her eyes. She said it made her look fat and only wore it when it was really cold. I hadn't realized how much I missed everything about her—even the stuff I always teased her about: her supercurly hair, the splash of teeny freckles over her nose, her funky clogs that she was wearing now. She stood in the doorway for a moment looking at me.

She looked so serious, I just wanted to see a smile, so I blinked to let her know I was awake, I was okay. She walked in and sat in the chair next to the bed. "Hi," she said quietly, looking down.

Oh shit.

No eye contact.

This was bad. The last time she pulled this no-eye-contact thing with me was when we broke up, when that dork from her lit class was asking her out. She met me at the bleachers after school and gave me the news. Looking down at her shoes the whole time, she told me this guy wanted to go out with her, he was writing her poems. God, I wanted to kill that guy so bad. Who does something like that with someone else's girlfriend? An asshole, that's who. He deserved to get his ass kicked. But Allie made me swear not to hurt the jerk. She just wanted some time "to think." To figure out what she really wanted. It was about her, her decision; he didn't have anything to do with it. That's what she said anyhow.

I walked home numb and played Xbox for about three hours with Mike, not talking. She sent me an e-mail that night, but I deleted it before I even read it. I was over it. I had been dumped. She broke my heart. Damn.

Looking at her now, my heart just squeezed shut. How could she do this to me again—now, while I'm like this?

"So, um, how are you?" she said awkwardly, still not

looking at me. A nurse walked in behind her, startling us both. "Sorry, just here for a quick check, then I'll leave you two alone." She adjusted my IV tube and looked at my chart, writing something. "You can hold his hand if you want, you know," she said to Allie.

"Oh, that's okay," Allie said, too quickly. She kept her hands folded in her lap.

As soon as the nurse left, Allie cleared her throat. I already knew what was coming next. She finally looked at my face, her blue eyes locking on mine, then she looked down again. "Your mom called me; she wanted me to come and see you again. She said you were doing better, that the doctors say you're doing better." She glanced up again at me. "West . . ." I could see tears on her face, her nose running. She grabbed a tissue from the box next to the bed and rubbed her nose.

"I'm sorry I haven't been here for a little bit. You know the weather has been really bad, and we've got winter finals. . . ." She stopped herself. Yeah, that's right: We didn't have winter finals. She did. I suddenly had this horrible vision of her studying with that poem-writing prick at her house, sitting on her bed like we used to do.

She looked down at her hands in her lap and took a deep breath. "But that's not why I haven't been here," she said quietly. "The truth is, I think about you all the time, West. All the things I want to say to you. But . . ." She closed her eyes. "Then I get here. And this hospital, this whole place . . . I don't know if I can do this, if I can come here anymore." She put her face into her hands and cried quietly. I wanted to reach out and touch her hair, tell her it would be okay. If she would just hold my hand for a second, I could teach her how I'm blinking for yes and no, and we could talk. I needed to ask for time, a few days to understand what was going on, how bad things really were. I had only been awake for a few days, maybe a week, and here she was, ready to dump me again.

Allie looked up and I thought for a second that maybe she had heard my thoughts. "I have to go, okay? I'm sorry." I shut my eyes and hoped for her to touch my hand, my face, my shoulder. I just wanted to feel her; it didn't have to be a kiss, just anything. But when I opened my eyes, she was gone.

From what she had said, she'd visited me here before, maybe when I was unconscious. How many times had she been here? I tried to console myself: She didn't say for sure she wasn't coming back. It wasn't over. She didn't say we were broken up, she just said she couldn't deal with the hospital, with the way things were now. So there was still a chance.

I lay there thinking about Allie and replaying how she dumped me before—and how I won her back. It took a long time and a lot of work. I had to show her I was the right guy for her. I listened to her and gave her the space she wanted and it all worked out. But how was I going to do it this time? I watched as the sun went down outside the window. A nurse went down the hall with a cart, and the sounds of the wheels yanked me back into the world of the living just in time for my mom to walk into the room. I had tears on my face that I couldn't wipe away, but Mom took a tissue and got them for me right away. "Hey, sweetie." She leaned over me, kissed my forehead. "How are you?" I blinked no for *not good*.

"I heard that you had a bad night. Bad dreams again?" I blinked yes and hoped that she could understand the code. She seemed to get it—the nurses must have explained, or maybe I had been communicating like this before, but I just forgot.

"I'll tell them it's okay to give you a sedative for night-time so that you won't have any more dreams like that." I didn't really want to be all drugged up, because it made the passage of time and everything else so confusing, but I also didn't want to have those nightmares anymore. Maybe it was better to be on the meds, at least until I could get to a place where I knew better what was going on, what was real, and what wasn't.

Mom reached through the bars of the bed and held my hand. She smiled, and for a minute, she just looked out the window, at the dusky sky. Then she squeezed my hand. "So

Friday's a big day, you know. We've finally got an appointment with Dr. Louis. He's the one I told you about last week—he's an expert in your type of injury and he's going to come examine you. Dad's going to take the day off, too, so we can both be here. I just know he's going to have good news for us."

I squeezed her hand back to let her know I understood. Maybe she had told me about this doctor before; I didn't remember, but her plan sounded good. I wanted to know exactly what was wrong with me and how to fix it. Then I could work on getting Allie back, getting to school, everything.

"Do you want to hear some *Harry Potter*?" she asked. "Oh, I talked to Allie, she told me they are reading *A Separate Peace* in English class right now. Should I get a copy of that and read it to you instead? I don't want you to fall too far behind."

I thought about it. I'd rather get lost in the fantasy world of Harry Potter for now, so I blinked no.

"I thought you'd probably want *Harry Potter*—I know, I know, you're too old for it now, but I just remember how much fun we had reading those books when you were younger." I could hear her voice catch. I remember, too, I wanted to tell her. I remember.

"Anyhow, the other book is a school assignment, so maybe I'll pick it up," Mom said, composing herself. She opened the drawer and took out *Harry Potter*, starting a chapter later in the book than where Olivia had left off. So now I had two people reading me the same book, but from different sections. Mom was already halfway through—she must have started days or weeks ago? She read a chapter, but to be honest, I was only half listening. My mind was on Allie, this new doctor, and trying to figure out exactly how long I had been here. When she closed the book, it was dark out and she looked tired. "Enough for tonight; more tomorrow, okay, sweetie? And in two days, we'll see Dr. Louis, and then we'll know more." She kissed my forehead and picked up her bag and jacket. "I will see you in the morning," she promised. "I love you, West," she said seriously, looking right into my eyes. I could see her memory, then, of sitting on my bed together, reading *Harry Potter*. Back when I was just a kid, before I even started biking. Before all of this. "You know how much I love you."

I just blinked to let her know her message was received. She smiled and walked out the door.

I looked at the doorway for the longest time, waiting for the nurse or Olivia to come. I guess she had already been by today, and I had a lot of visitors, but I was still looking forward to seeing her. I was hoping she would come and bring the board. I had an important question for her, and I knew only she had the patience to wait for me while I wrote it. After a while, Nurse Norris showed up, and the night shift had begun already.

"Sorry to do this to you at bedtime, but the doctor says he still wants you rolled," Norris explained. She secured the strap that ran over my forehead and undid the locks on either side of bed, rotating me so that I was facing the wall. "We won't have to do this too much longer, okay?" She looked at my face when she talked to me, which I appreciated, especially after what had happened with Allie.

"What is going on here, mister?" My hand was loose in the binding, where Olivia had not strapped it back in right. "You trying to break out of here? Your mom probably did that to hold your hand." She secured my hand and then went back to the foot of the bed to check my chart. "Oh boy, they are bringing out the big guns, look at this dosage. Okay, if that's what the doctor ordered." She prepared a syringe of something and pumped it into my IV. Again I felt the cold liquid dash though the veins in my arm. Then, after a second, the warm feeling took over, and I felt amazing. Suddenly, I wasn't worrying about Allie, or anything. Whatever this stuff was, it felt about eight hundred times better than being drunk. I drifted off thinking about the kegger at Mike's place where I first met Allie, when I first had the balls to talk to her.

She was sitting up on the kitchen counter and she was sort of dressed up. I had to think of something to say to her, something to start a conversation. I'd been seeing her at drama after school for weeks and trying to find a way to talk to her. We didn't have any of the same classes. I had no idea who her friends were. It was impossible.

I just went over and stood sort of close to where she was, hoping something would happen, like osmosis, and somehow we would end up talking. One of her friends was up on the counter with her. Their heads were close together, and they were talking about something. I followed their eyes to the living room, where Mike was standing on the coffee table. He looked like he was pretending to be on a surfboard, except he had a beer in each hand. Allie and her friend did not look amused.

"If you want a surfing lesson, I think Mike is teaching them for free in the living room," I said, trying to be funny.

"We live five hours from the nearest ocean. I think I'll pass," her friend snarked back, and Allie laughed. But then she took mercy on me.

"You're friends with him, right?" she asked me. "With Mike?"

"Yeah, we hang out."

"But you're also in drama?" She looked a little confused, like someone who was friends with Mike couldn't also be into the drama club.

Her friend slid down off the counter. "It's too loud in here. I'm going outside, you coming?"

Allie shook her head, and her friend shrugged and walked off.

I looked back at Allie and just stood there. I couldn't think of anything to say. Should I give her a compliment? Tell her she looked pretty tonight? No, that would come out wrong. Like she didn't usually look pretty. The music suddenly seemed to be louder, more obnoxious.

"So . . . ," I finally said. Then I just stood there, like an idiot, waiting for something cool to come out of my mouth.

"So, drama?" she asked when it was clear I was totally floundering.

"Oh, that." I shook my head. "I built the bike ramp, the one at the park next to school. So Mrs. Herbert asked me to help out with the sets, just building and stuff, you know." I tried to growl like a caveman and added, "Power tools."

Allie smiled. "Don't put yourself down. I saw the drawings you did for the sets, they're amazing. You're really talented. Have you had a lot of art classes?" She met my eyes in a serious way that made me wish I hadn't had three beers already.

"Uh, no, I don't know. . . ." I looked across the room at Mike, who was now standing on one leg, using the beers to help him balance, doing a *Karate Kid* move. He had a crowd of admirers around him, the usual gang of idiots, cheering him on.

"How is it that you guys are friends?" Allie asked, and I was glad she changed the subject.

"That's a long story." I didn't want to get into it. "You ask a lot of questions, you know that?"

Now it was Allie's turn to blush. "Do I?" Then she laughed.

I mocked her high voice, asking, "Do I?"

She kept laughing at my impression of her, which I took as a good sign that she wasn't a bitch and didn't take herself too seriously. "Okay, I guess I do. I'm sorry. Now it's your turn—ask me anything."

I stood next to her, so close I could touch her bare leg if I moved my hand an inch. I met her eyes and leaned in so I wouldn't have to yell. "Do you have a boyfriend?" I only had the courage to ask because I already knew the answer. I'd done my homework.

"No." She didn't flinch.

"Can I get you a beer?"

"That's two questions," she said, smiling. "But okay." The beer made her cheeks turn pink, which was the cutest thing I'd ever seen. After that, we never stopped talking. God, she was so beautiful, I couldn't even believe she was speaking to me. That was the night when everything changed. Suddenly, I had a girlfriend. Allie. I wanted her, I went after her, and I got her. I almost couldn't believe my good luck. I should have known it couldn't last.

Chapter 5

I walk into the school with Allie. It's winter and it's cold and she's got her puffy coat on. I'm trying to squeeze her like a marshmallow and pick her up. "Stop it!" she squeals, slapping my hands away. We go to my locker first, and I see Mike. He's got a skater hat pulled down over his rowdy red hair, the kind of hat you're not supposed to wear in school. "Dude, I thought you were in the hospital," he says, slapping me a high five.

"Didn't you hear? The doctors were wrong, he's totally fine," Allie says quickly.

"That is excellent," Mike says. "But are you ready for midterms?"

Then it hits me: I totally forgot to study. I open my backpack, but it's full of hospital stuff: syringes, tubes, bandages, the straps that held me on the bed. "Oh man, I think I brought the wrong bag."

Mike's laughing. "Uh, I hate to say this, but you are gonna fail big time."

"Maybe you just go home and pretend you're sick, you don't have to take the tests today," Allie says.

"Yeah, you're not really dressed for school," Mike points out. "Just go to the office. I'll tell you what's on the test later."

"Mike!" Allie says. "That's cheating."

The bell sounds and they walk away together and leave me standing in the hallway alone. I look down and see that he's right, I'm not dressed for school. I'm wearing my hospital gown. I still have an IV attached to my hand, there's blood running down my arm, pooling on the floor.

———

I woke up to a nurse taping a new IV down on my hand. She didn't talk to me or look at me, so I guess she didn't notice that I was awake. She adjusted the IV bag and left before I was really awake. The drugs they were giving me at night were insane. I had also been rotated again, onto my back, but I didn't remember who did that, or when. I didn't mind—the faster time went by, the faster I could get to Friday and see this doctor and hear what was really going on with me.

By midmorning, I felt a little bit more normal. The

dream was still haunting me, but at least it wasn't a creepy one, and at least I didn't really have midterms today. I was wondering about Mike, and if he had ever come by to visit me, when Olivia rolled into the room with her IV stand.

"Hello, Prince Charming," she said. "Good night last night, huh? I didn't hear anything from over here, so I'm guessing you slept like a baby."

I looked at her hands and was bummed to see that she didn't have the whiteboard with her. How was I going to talk to her without it? "Don't look so sad, I know what you're looking for." She opened the drawer by my bed and took out the board. "Wanna chat?" she joked.

She reached down to where her own IV went into her arm. It was attached to a piece of plastic that went under her skin and was there permanently. I'd heard the nurses call it a shunt. She capped the line and pulled it out of the needle, leaving the shunt in place, but cutting off the flow. Just like that, she wasn't attached to her pole anymore. "Liquid nutrition has lots of calories. A lady has to watch her figure, you know." She smiled and I noticed she had put on some lip gloss or something. Was that for me?

"Here we go." She undid the strap on my right wrist and put the pen into my hand. I squeezed hard and set my mind to work. I had just one question for her. She held the board close to me and I started writing. After a few lines, she took the board away. "*H*, and a . . . what is this letter? Did you write *Hi* again?"

I blinked no and she looked the board more closely. "Is this someone's name?"

I blinked no and motioned with my hand that I wanted to write more. "Oh, is it *how*?"

I blinked yes. "Okay." She wiped the board and put it back by my hand. This word was longer, but didn't take me as long to write because I was getting the hang of this.

"Love?" Olivia asked and raised an eyebrow, looking skeptical. Without looking at me, she got it. "How long," she said. "A question, how long—?"

I blinked yes.

"How long have we been here. Gosh, I don't know." She looked up at the ceiling like she was thinking hard. "A year or so, I guess."

No, no, no.

I dropped the pen on the floor and felt vomit roll up my throat.

That wasn't possible. My heart monitor started to go beep quickly.

"Okay, oh my God, calm down, don't have a heart attack! I was kidding." Olivia laughed, showing her little dark-white teeth. "I've been here forever. You? It's been like a month, maybe. Or like three weeks. Not long. God, I thought you would appreciate a little joke! I guess you really didn't know, huh?"

I could tell she felt bad, but I was also starting to realize that Olivia had a real dark streak. She could be supersweet, but there was a hard side to her that reminded me of the girls at school I really couldn't stand, the cheerleaders and their friends. "The Mean Girls," Allie called them.

"I saw that your girlfriend was here yesterday. Pretty girl." So that's what this was about. That's why she didn't come to see me yesterday after Allie left.

Was Olivia jealous?

"Did you guys go out a long time?"

I blinked yes, realizing that she was putting our relationship in the past tense, probably because she had heard the whole conversation from her room. It pissed me off to think that she was sitting over there listening to Allie talk to me. It wasn't any of her business.

"Well, you should know, when she was checking in yesterday, the nurse asked her if she was your girlfriend and you know what she said? That you were friends. She said, 'Well, we're *friends*, we go to the same school.' Sorry, but she seems kind of like a bitch to me. You're better off without her."

When Olivia tried to put the pen back into my hand, I wouldn't take it, instead letting it drop to the floor.

"What's wrong? Don't tell me you're mad," Olivia scolded. She tried again with the pen, pushing my fingers closed around it, but I wouldn't play along. "Look, I'm not the one who broke up with you. I'm just trying to help you."

When she took her hand off mine, I let the pen drop to the floor again. I wasn't about to cooperate.

"Fine." She stood in a huff and shoved the board into the drawer, slamming it shut. "Call me when you get your period, okay?" She stormed out, sliding the wall shut between our rooms with a dramatic slam.

A second later, I heard it slide open again, and her footsteps around my bed. "I forgot this stupid thing." She snatched her IV pole and tried to make another dramatic exit but the wheels caught on the side of my bed. "Dang it!" she stopped. "This is dumb. Let's not be mad, okay? You're the only person I can talk to here. I don't want you to hate me." She fiddled with her IV tubing and reattached the shunt. She was being too rough in her anger. I saw her face flinch in pain as she pushed the tubes together. "Ouch! This sucks. This whole place sucks. I'm sorry that I joked around like that, and I'm sorry about your girlfriend. I guess I've sort of forgotten how to be friends with someone, I've been in here so long." I didn't move, didn't blink.

"Okay? See you tomorrow?" She stood defiantly in front of me, waiting for an answer. She was looking me right in the eye, not at her feet, not at the window. At me. Really looking at me. That was better than most of the other folks who came to see me in this state. Unlike Allie, Olivia only knew me like this, she didn't expect me to be anything else. And if she was willing to be friends, I wasn't really in a position to be choosy.

Reluctantly I blinked yes. Olivia gave me a weak smile, then she went back to her room, closing the door softly behind her.

Chapter 6

This time it's snowing all around us. I'm watching them struggle on the ground. She's pushing him. STOP IT PLEASE. I want to help her, but I can't. I turn to run, but I can't move, my legs are tied together. I see him pull his fist back to punch her. I know I should stop him, but I don't. I can't. I can't move. I watch and feel so sick. The thud of his fist on her face, over and over. I'm throwing up, I feel it coming up my throat. "Don't you scratch me!" he says, punching her again. She's not screaming now. She's quiet. He stands, looks at her, kicks her body. She doesn't move. He spits, then turns to see me standing there. I'm right next to him. I see his face. He looks at me like he doesn't care I'm seeing him, seeing what he has done. "Don't worry about her," he says. "She's a waste of time." He's right in my face now; I can see a tattoo on his hand as he brings it up. I feel his bloody fingers touching my cheek. *Oh God no.*

———

When I woke up, the bright winter sun was pouring into the room. I was still having the dream, but I guess not having heart palpitations that would send a nurse into my room thanks to the heavy-duty bedtime drugs. As I lay there, something came to me. Why was I having this dream, the same dream, over and over again? I had never had dreams like this before I was in the hospital—I'd never even had the same dream twice. Now I couldn't stop having this dream, about this guy. It just didn't make sense. It must have something to do with being here, with the hospital or this room, but I couldn't figure out what it was.

I drifted back to sleep and when I awoke, the day was half-gone. I remembered the dream, a little bit, and remembered that I had a theory about it, but what was it? I was trying to sort it out, because when I had woken up earlier, it all made sense somehow, but now that I was really awake, it didn't come together again like it had before.

"It's Thursday!" I heard from the accordion wall. I could hear it sliding open. "Tomorrow's Friday, you know," Olivia said, waltzing into my room like yesterday had never happened. "Remember? Your mom is bringing an expert doctor guy to examine you. I'm curious to hear what he's gonna say."

I felt myself soften to her. Besides, it wasn't like I could kick her out.

"You excited? Your mom has been building this up since you got here. I heard her tell you one night that your parents paid for this guy to fly into town, so he's a big deal." Olivia undid her IV tube from her shunt again and pushed the pole to the side of the room. She curled up on the other bed.

"You're lucky to have parents who care so much about you, you know that, right? My mom is here about once a week, if I'm lucky. And if she's off with one of her new boyfriends, it can be more like two weeks. Last time she showed up, I wouldn't even look at her." She stopped for a second. "Your mom is here every day, and if she hears that you had a bad night, she's here before she goes to work, too. So I guess you had some bad dreams last night, huh?"

I blinked yes. Then no.

"You did have one or not?" she asked me, sitting up on the bed.

I blinked yes.

"Really? So I wanted to ask you, but I think I already know the answer. Are these dreams about your accident, the bike accident?"

I blinked no, then yes. There was one dream like that, I think, but mostly they were about the street, the guy with the bloody knuckles, the girl he was hurting. I could remember having it at least twice, but it seemed so familiar to me, I think I had it a few more times than that. When I'm walking on that street, I know I've been there before, seen what happens before.

"So you're having dreams—nightmares—about something else?"

I blinked yes.

Olivia hopped off the bed and pulled open the drawer, grabbing the whiteboard. "I assume we're talking again?" She smiled.

When I blinked yes, she quickly undid the strap on my right arm and slid the pen into my hand. "We don't have a ton of time before the next check."

She held the board close enough for me to write on, but I paused. How could I get this across in as few words as possible? I started with a *B* and moved on from there. It took about a minute. When Olivia looked at the board, she studied it carefully. I had never had neat handwriting, but trying to write when you're lying down, strapped in, and using just one slightly paralyzed hand is not the way to good penmanship.

"Bad?" she finally said. "As in, you're having *bad* dreams?" She looked puzzled.

I blinked no. "More?" She wiped the board and put it back by my hand. This time I wrote just one word.

"*Man*. You're having dreams about a bad man?" I blinked yes and motioned for the board. I wrote *room* this time.

"You're having bad dreams, about a bad man . . . in this room?" Olivia looked terrified. "You mean, like a ghost—in *here*? Oh my God, I knew it! I knew this room was haunted!"

I blinked no quickly. "What do you mean, I didn't get it right?" She put the board back by my hand, but I was at a loss. The dreams weren't happening in the room, but I knew the room or the hospital was somehow connected to the dreams. Hospital was too long a word, it would take forever to write. Instead I wrote *not in*. It took me a minute and I was feeling totally exhausted when I got done, I dropped the pen.

Olivia picked it up without saying a word and looked at the board.

"*Not in*. Not in . . . here? Not in the room." I blinked yes.

"Why did you write *room* then? I don't get it. *Bad, man, room, not in.* I'm just trying to figure out what you're saying." She sounded a little exasperated with me. She glanced at the clock and quickly slid the board into the drawer. "Oh crap. To be continued," she said, grabbing her IV pole. As she went around my bed, she quickly kissed my cheek. "I'm glad we're friends again," she whispered, sliding the door shut.

About thirty seconds after she left, Nurse Norris walked in. Olivia knew the timing of the nursing checks down to the minute.

"Good evening, sir," Nurse Norris said, and smiled. "Now, since your mom was here this morning, she is not going to make it back over tonight, but she wanted me to remind you that you've got a doctor coming tomorrow. Both your parents are gonna be here." She looked into my face and then shined her flashlight in my eyes. "You heard me?" she asked, and I blinked yes. "I know you did," she said softly. "Okay then, let's give you a little spin so you look good for the doctor tomorrow. We don't want you all full of fluid, do we?"

She pulled the strap over my forehead, something I was really starting to hate, and then rotated the bed so that I was facing the window. The sun was just setting and the sky was a salmon pink, the puffy clouds like cotton candy. It looked so cool, I caught myself wishing I could text Allie and tell her to look outside. My chest clenched up at the thought of her, and at the thought of using a phone again to text anyone. Where was my phone anyhow? Who would I call if I could hold it? Who were my friends now? I was praying this doctor tomorrow was going to have some good news for me.

"Would you look at that sunset?" Nurse Norris sighed deeply. "I'm always thinking about God when I see something like that. It's just too beautiful to be an accident." She clicked the bed into place and noticed again that my arm strap was undone—Olivia had completely forgotten to redo it this time. "Your mom . . . got to talk to her about this," she murmured as she redid the strap and secured my arm. "Well, I'll be right back with your night-night cocktail, handsome."

She left the room and I stared at the sunset for a long time. She was right, it was too beautiful to be an accident. Especially tonight. Maybe this meant I wouldn't have the nightmare. Maybe it meant that the doctor tomorrow was going to tell me something encouraging. I could still feel the place on my cheek where Olivia had kissed me. It felt good. I stared hard at the pink sky and recited the Lord's Prayer in my head.

Thy kingdom come, Thy will be done.

Maybe.

Chapter 7

When I opened my eyes, I was surprised to see the sun pouring into the room. It was a new day. It was Friday. I hadn't had the dream, I hadn't had any dreams at all. The clock on the wall read 10:25. I hadn't slept the whole day away in a fog. This was all good, things were looking up. I waited to see who was going to come in, what time my appointment was. When did Mom say? I couldn't remember, or maybe she hadn't told me.

The day nurse came in, the one who wasn't Norris and also wasn't nice. Not that she was mean, but she didn't ever talk to me, or anyone. Just did her job and left. I made eye contact with her a few times, but she always looked away. She checked my chart, adjusted some tubes, pressed a few buttons on the ventilator, and walked out. Why would someone who hates people so much go into nursing anyhow?

By the time the clock read 11:30 a.m., my eyelids were getting pretty heavy just listening to the rhythmic sound of the respirator pumping in and out. No visit from Olivia, no Mom, no Dad, no doctor. It was Friday, right? What if it was Saturday already and I just didn't know it? I drifted off worrying and awoke with a start, feeling like I was falling backward down a staircase. I opened my eyes, suddenly terrified—something was wrong. I wasn't in my bed. I was on my back, staring at something white and plastic right over my head. My heart started racing. Was I dead? I could see that there was light down by my feet, like I was inside a big tube. Must be an X-ray or something. Mom's voice was talking to me through a speaker by my head. "West, you're okay, we're just doing an MRI for the doctor. You'll be out of there soon, okay? They're almost done." Then Dad's voice, quietly: "Jesus, Cath, he can't even hear you; leave it alone, would you?"

"You don't know that—how would you like to wake up in there, not knowing where the hell you are?"

Divorced five years and still at it.

"West, they are almost done, then you'll be back in your room. Just hang tight," Mom went on.

"It's going to get a little loud again, so I'm going to switch this off," I heard someone say. Something clicked and the speaker she was talking over cut out. Then came a sound hammering all around me, a constant pounding and clicking around the tube I was in. It wasn't hurting me, and I couldn't feel it, but it sounded like someone was beating a hammer right over my head. *Bang, bang, bang, bang.* No one could sleep through that.

The banging stopped for a minute, then started up again in a different place, over to the right of me. Then they stopped again, and started on the left.

"How ya doing in there?" I heard a male voice say, then some mumbling. The speaker clicked off again. Suddenly the bed I was on jerked a little and started to move forward, bringing me out of the tube. When I looked up, there were two guys standing over me, both in uniforms. Maybe they were male nurses.

"On my count," one of them said. "One, two, and up." They lifted me by a sheet and put me back onto my own bed but left the wrist and arm straps undone. They moved the respirator and IV tubes from outside the MRI machine back over to the poles on my bed.

"He's first floor, room 201," one of the guys said as the other one wheeled me out into the hallway. There was Mom and Dad and another guy in a suit, maybe the doctor Mom told me about. He looked older, with gray hair.

"As soon as we can get those other test results," he was saying, "we'll know more, but from what I've seen, I suspect that he has a similar case to the one I described to you over the phone." All of them were walking behind me as the two nurses wheeled my bed back down the hall. I couldn't remember ever being outside of my room before. The nurses' station on my right, then other rooms, some with open doors, some closed.

We stopped at the first door past the nurses' station and went in through the wide doorway. My bed was pushed against the wall, headfirst like it usually was, and the nurse put his foot on something down by the wheels, locking it into place. "Home sweet home, buddy," he said, and attached a chart back to the foot of the bed as my parents walked in behind him. The guy kind of reminded me of Mike—bright-red hair, superwhite skin. Except he kept his hair short, not shaggy like Mike. "The nurse will be in to make sure he's settled," he said as he left. I guess he wasn't a nurse, but an orderly.

Behind my parents, the older man in the suit walked in—the famous doctor.

"How soon could you perform the surgery?" Dad asked him.

"I would have to consult my schedule, and of course, I will need to see his test results to be sure, but I think . . ."

Mom cut him off. "If we decide to go that route."

"Yes, of course, you can consider other options, but I would encourage you to make a decision quickly. The longer he remains in this condition, the more damage that is being done."

"What does that mean?" Dad asked. "They told us that he was stabilized before we even moved him here."

"Yes, stabilized, in this condition. But his immune system will continue to attack the foreign object pressuring his spinal column, and that can cause further damage."

"We have to talk this over with West, too." Mom looked over at me and moved to the side of the bed, taking my hand.

"He's seventeen, we're making this decision for him," Dad said. "If it's up to me, he's having the surgery."

"Well it isn't up to you, it's *our* decision," Mom said forcefully. "As a family." She squeezed my hand.

The doctor took in a deep breath and looked uncomfortable. "Perhaps we should take this conversation outside?"

My parents had always made an effort not to fight in front of me. Even when stuff got really bad with the divorce, they would always take it in another room, or Mom would say, "Let's discuss this later," and march off. I realized they were doing the same thing now—a fight was brewing, but they would have it in the hallway. I wished they would just keep talking here because I wanted to know if this doctor could fix me, and how fast. From what he was saying, I couldn't really tell.

A few minutes later, Mom came back in and leaned

over me. "Well, I've got some really good news for you. The doctor says you can sit up now and be in a wheelchair, so we can go outside and go for walks and everything. Won't that be nice?" Mom pushed the hair back from my forehead. I blinked yes, it would be nice to feel the sun on my face, to get outside. But being in a wheelchair didn't sound like good news. That was his advice? It made me nervous. Once they got me in one, did that mean I would ever get out of it again? She wasn't saying and I couldn't ask. "And you'll be in a different type of bed, you don't need to be rotated around anymore. Just a regular bed."

Dad walked into the room behind her. "Okay, big guy, I've got a flight to catch." He took my other hand. It was sort of nice, having both of my parents there at once, each holding one hand. It was like I was a little kid again. I didn't expect to see both of my parents in the same place at the same time until graduation.

Dad let go of my hand and glanced up at Mom. "Sorry about before; it's just that I really can't stand to see him like this a moment longer, it's literally killing me. The risks are all worth it, you know that."

"I'm not going to discuss this in front of him. I'll call you tonight," she said firmly.

Dad nodded, looking sad. "Fine. That will give us both a little time to think things over. I'll talk to you then." He reached over and touched the back of her hand, giving it a squeeze. She looked as surprised as I was. Dad, being nice to Mom? Things were serious.

When the door closed behind him, Mom pulled over the chair and sat next to me. "I'm sure you heard enough to understand what's going on. There's a surgery Dr. Louis thinks could really help you. It's risky. And to be honest with you, I'm not even over your accident yet. I'm so happy that you're alive, I'm not sure I want to take another chance on losing you." Tears were quietly flowing down her cheeks, but she didn't let go of my hand to wipe them away. "All the doctors and nurses agree that you are young and so healthy and you have so much going for you, maybe the risks are not that great, considering . . . well, considering the alternative." Mom sniffled. "No reason to get ahead of ourselves; he'll call us tonight with the results of your MRI and we'll know more."

There was a quick knock at the door, and Nurse Norris walked in. "How's he doing? Okay after that big adventure this afternoon?" Her smile changed the whole room and I felt like everything was going to be okay.

"He's fine; not sure about me," Mom said.

Norris handed her the box of tissues. "Honey, it's going to be okay, it really is." She picked up my chart, then glanced at Mom again. "Go home and get yourself some rest. I've got things under control. You know he's my favorite patient."

Mom let go of my hand and kissed my forehead. "You were a brave boy today. I'm proud of you."

I didn't know what was so brave about lying in a tube for a few minutes, but if Mom wanted to say something nice, I was willing to hear it.

She lingered in the door for a second until Nurse Norris said, "Go on now, beat the traffic. We'll see you tomorrow."

She hummed as she leaned over me and checked my respirator tube. "Well, for once the X-ray tech did not screw things up too badly." She straightened the IV tube from one arm, then put both of my arms under their straps. "This is the last night we're rotating you; Doctor says you're ready for range-of-motion work starting tomorrow. That's exciting, huh?" She pulled my sheet up across my chest and folded it down carefully like she did every night. "I'll try to see that you get the really pretty physical therapist, okay?" She gave me a quick wink. She turned the light down on her way out, leaving the room lit with the warm glow of the setting winter sun.

Why would they start physical therapy now, before the surgery? That didn't make any sense, unless my mom had decided she really didn't want me to have the surgery. I wished I could have heard everything they were talking about in the hallway with the doctor, so that I could be part of the discussion. It was my body, and my life, after all.

But maybe there was a way to find out what they had

talked out after they left my room, even the stuff they didn't want me to hear. There was one person I was sure had heard every word and probably couldn't wait to tell me: Olivia.

Chapter 8

'm riding to Allie's house; I know this route, this sidewalk and street by heart. It's two miles. The section of sidewalk where the giant oak trees have buckled the pavement is my favorite. Speed plus cracked pavement equals air: a simple equation. My backpack is heavy: history book, assigned reading, notebooks. Every time I get air, my backpack goes up—weightless—then slams back down onto my shoulders, pulling on my neck. It hurts a little, but I'd rather get jumps than worry about my backpack, so I keep going— faster, higher, harder.

We've got work to do, and I know Allie will make sure we do it, but I want to wrap my arms around her and just lie there on her bed with her for a minute or two.

Then I'm there, I'm on Allie's bed, the light-green quilt,

the pillow that smells like her hair. But she's not next to me, I'm alone.

"Allie?" Maybe she's in the bathroom or something. I try to roll over and check the clock by her bed but I can't. I'm strapped in. *No, this isn't real*, I tell myself. *This is a bad dream. I'm okay.* The room is dark. The door opens and Nurse Norris comes in. Her face looks happy, but then suddenly changes. "What are you doing in here?" she says, looking at the other side of the bed. I turn my eyes and see the guy, the bad guy, the one who attacked that girl. He's standing next to the bed. He smiles and I can see his teeth, snarled and stained. Suddenly, he lunges over my body and grabs Norris by the throat. She turns and tries to get away from him, pulling him with her. The weight of his body is across my legs, I can feel him crawling over me to get to her. He scrambles over me, and then he's on top of her on the floor, punching her, and she's screaming.

———

"Look at you, ready to go this morning! I like your attitude," chirped a woman with really short blond hair, standing next to my bed. "And let's take the left leg again, in and up, in and up." She bent my left leg at the knee, then extended it up straight. I could see the road rash still on my shins from the accident. I guess I hadn't looked at my legs since I woke up. They looked terrible, dark brown scabs to the knee, like hamburger had been spread over my legs. This must be physical therapy. She put my leg back down, then picked up my left arm. "Now, let's get to work on your upper body."

She was pretty in an older-lady sort of way: not as old as Mom but not young enough to be hot. If this was the pretty therapist that Norris promised me, I wondered what the other ones looked like.

She pulled my arm up and around in circles and it sort of felt awesome. I couldn't lift my arms so to have someone else do it was good. Her hands were soft and warm and she was holding me, guiding my arm. "That's it, perfect, keep your arm straight now, don't bend at the elbow, nice and straight. See? You just straightened it yourself, nice job!" I had sent a signal to my arm to be straight, like she said, but I wasn't sure if it got there. Guess it did. "Other arm now," she said, moving over to my other side and lifting that arm. "And out now," she said, extending my arm toward the wall. "Controlled movements, as much as you can." She leaned in and talked really loud, close to my ear. The problem is not my hearing, I wanted to tell her. The problem is everything else.

As she moved my limbs around, the dream came back to me. Allie's room, Nurse Norris and the guy. What did it mean? Why did I keep dreaming about this guy? Then I had a horrifying realization: What if I was seeing the future? What if I banged my head so badly in the accident that now I could see what was about to happen? I remembered a TV movie where that happened to someone. He was hit by lightning and got psychic powers. Did that mean that Nurse Norris or Allie was going to be attacked by this guy? What color hair did the girl have in the other dream, the one where he was hurting that girl? I couldn't remember, couldn't focus on anything in the dream but him.

The therapist pulled the bed up into a sitting position really slowly. "We don't want you to get light-headed." When I was almost sitting up straight, I did feel a little queasy. Weird what will happen if you lie down for a few weeks.

"We'll stay like this for a couple of minutes. This is part of your therapy. I know that sounds funny, but it's going to take you some practice to get used to sitting up again." She raised the bed a little higher, so that I was sitting straight up. I realized this wasn't the bed I was in before. Sometime in the night, or early this morning, they had moved me into a different bed, one without the straps.

"And there you go. You're going to stay just like this for about ten minutes. I'm going to get your chair now, and we're going for a walk, okay?" She kept talking really loud like I was a little kid. I blinked yes at her and she left to get the chair.

She hadn't been gone a few moments when Olivia opened the accordion wall between our rooms. "*Pssssst, is* your lady friend gone?" She giggled, then stopped suddenly. "Geez, you're sitting up? Seriously?" She walked into the room, taking a quick look around and pulling her IV stand in behind her when she saw the coast was clear. "New bed, too? So, who is this miracle worker and what exactly did she do to you, huh?" She plopped into the chair and pulled it over. "Tell me everything!" She put her hand under her chin like she was really waiting for me to tell her something entertaining. I had missed her yesterday. It was just nice to see her face.

"Blink once if physical therapy is as boring as it sounds," she said, pulling her knees up under her robe and curling into the chair.

I blinked once. "More boring than a sponge bath?"

I blinked once, then twice. Undecided. I sort of liked the sponge bath.

"We have a lot of catching up to do, mister. I'm dying to hear what your doctor said, good news?" she whispered.

Shit, did that mean she hadn't heard everything the doctor and my parents had said in the hallway yesterday? I had been counting on her filling in the blanks for me.

"I was trying my best to 'accidentally' go down the hall when the specialist was here, but I couldn't manage it. Believe it or not, my mom showed up yesterday, right when they took you for your MRI. She wanted to hang out forever; she's going on a cruise so she'll be gone for two weeks."

Olivia shrugged. "Bad timing, I missed the whole thing. So fill me in, good news? Blink once."

I blinked once, because I did consider it good news. I think it was.

"And did that chick just say she was going to get you a wheelchair?"

I blinked once.

"Wow, okay." Olivia was smiling and nodding her head, but she didn't look especially happy.

"Well, at least now I can take you on walks. We can go to the game room, watch TV. We'll be buddies!" she said jokingly. "Seriously, it will be fun. I'll make it fun. And before you know it, you'll be getting out of here." She stood up and looked down, busying herself with her IV pole so I couldn't see her face.

So that's what was bothering her. It was looking like I was getting better, getting out. The thought of being in this hospital for weeks—or months—like Olivia made my stomach turn. I did want to get out of here; I didn't look forward to playing UNO and watching TV with other sick kids. That's how Olivia and I were totally different. Sometimes it almost seemed like Olivia liked it here, even though she said she didn't.

Things suddenly felt awkward between us, like there was a secret we weren't talking about. "Well, have a nice walk with your lady friend." Olivia gave me a weak smile. "Guess

I'll catch you later, unless you're too fast for me." She pointed at me, quick draw with her fingers like a gun, then dropped her hand to her side. She stood like that, looking at me like she was thinking about something for a moment before she went back into her room and closed the partition softly. I had to see Olivia's unhappiness as a good thing. If she thought this was a step toward getting out of here, maybe it was. Maybe she knew more than she was saying.

The physical therapist walked back in with a male orderly I'd seen before, the guy with the red hair. "He looks good, right? He's been sitting for ten minutes, and his color is excellent. I think we can do this today," she said, taking my arms into her hands.

"Whatever you say," he murmured, and moved the chair over to the end of the bed. He put his foot near the back tire, putting the brakes on, before he lowered the arm rests on both sides.

"I'm Kim," she said loudly, looking into my face. "You remember me, right? I'm your physical therapist." God, she must really think I was totally gone upstairs; she was just in here a few minutes ago. I blinked yes with emphasis. "Okay, West, we're going to move you into the chair now." She hit a pedal by the bed and the bottom dropped away, leaving my feet dangling down so I was sitting up like I was in a chair.

The orderly moved over to one side of me and tucked

his hand under my thigh, while Kim did the same on the other side. They each had one hand on my back. "On my count," the guy said, "one, two, and—" They lifted me and with a quick turn to the side, they were able to put me into the chair easily. The guy snapped up the side arm rails and placed my hands into my lap. "Let me know when you need help getting him back in." The guy motioned to the bed with his head, then left the room.

Kim moved my IV bag to a pole on the chair and unhooked my respirator tube from the large machine next to the bed, quickly plugging it into something behind the chair. "Portable ventilator," she said, coming back around in front of me, "seems to all be working great. Your color looks good, you okay?" She looked into my face with such intensity, I blinked yes, and I really did. This felt just like sitting up in the bed, except I was lower to the ground. It did seem weird to finally be out of the bed, to be mobile. Kim crouched in front of the chair and placed my feet into the footrests on either side so they were up off the floor. I could feel her hands on my feet, on my lower leg, but it felt like I was wearing ski pants and boots, like something thick was in the way, even though I knew there wasn't. I knew my legs were bare, my feet too.

It was good to be looking out the door of my room from a different angle for the first time. This was a step in the right direction. Olivia was right to be worried; I was getting out of here. It was going to happen. I was done lying down, trapped on a bed, and I'd only been here a few weeks.

"Let's do this," Kim said, standing behind the chair and clicking the brake off. Even though I knew she couldn't see my face, I blinked yes—I was ready to go.

Chapter 9

I walk into Olivia's room and see that it's just like mine—a mirror image, except that she has a pile of magazines next to her bed and a small glass vase with pink roses. She's sitting on the bed with her back to me. Her head is down. She turns when she hears me, and her face lights up. "Hey," she says softly. She holds her hand out to me. I take it, and sit down next to her.

"Do you know what I love about you?" she says, looking out the window. "We don't have to talk and I know what you're thinking. You don't have to say a word." She stops to look at me. Her dark eyes lock on mine for a second, long enough to make my chest clench up. "I can tell what you're thinking right now." She smiles and looks down. "And the fact that you don't have to say it makes it true, makes it more real than anything. I know you feel it, too." Her hand comes up to my face, she runs her thumb over my lips and whispers my name. "West, West . . ."

———

"West," Olivia was whispering so hard she was practically hissing. "West, can I come in?" She didn't wait for an answer, not that I could give her one, just slid the divider open and walked in. I noticed she didn't have her IV stand. "So that Kim girl wore you out, huh?" she whispered. "Remember, she was the one pushing you, not the other way around." She pulled a chair close to the bed and curled up on the seat. "Oh, I saw you, cruising by my room, poppin' wheelies. A word of advice: no one likes a show-off." She smiled but I felt like something was wrong. Were we just kissing? Was I touching her? Was she touching me? It was so dark in my room. I looked to the clock and saw that it was close to three in the morning.

"I thought you wouldn't want to miss this opportunity," she said, looking at me more closely. "Come on, get with the program; rise and shine if you want to take a midnight stroll. Isn't this what we've been waiting for?"

And then I remembered, all in a rush. The physical therapist. The walk down the hall. Going by Olivia's room, and hoping she would come out and say hi, at least stand in the doorway to see me roll by. She didn't. Kim took me to the end of the hallway, by rows of rooms, most with their doors closed, a TV room with a daytime talk show playing at low volume to empty chairs. The glass doors at the end of the hall led to a sidewalk outside. "We'll tackle that tomorrow," Kim had said.

Now it was dark and Olivia was in my room. She pushed a button on the side of the bed and raised up the back slowly until I was sitting. "Do you want to do this?" I blinked yes, but I wasn't sure I knew what she was talking about, or if she knew what she was doing.

"I was watching everything," she whispered, as if reading my thoughts. "I know exactly what to do." She moved quietly over to the wheelchair sitting in the corner of the room and positioned it exactly where it needed to be, then hit the pedal to drop the bed under my feet. "Here's the tricky part—you need to lean over me, okay?" She moved in as if she was going to hug me, and a dream came back to me, Olivia touching my face. . . . She was touching me, moving my arm over her head, wrapping her right arm around my body, grabbing me under the arm. "Okay, lean in," she ordered, pulling me forward so the weight of my torso was on her back. She tipped back, and I thought she would fall headfirst onto the linoleum floor, but she was able to hold me, half hugging me, long enough to flop me back over and put me into the chair.

"You're fat," she joked, catching her breath. "No, seriously, that was easier than I thought. I'm stronger than I look, huh?" She moved the IV bag over the pole on the wheel-chair. "I told you I was a dancer," she said, taking a quick pirouette. Then she got serious, looking at the tube in my throat. "Okay, now what do we do about this?" That's when it hit me. I was sitting in a wheelchair for only the second time since my accident.

In the middle of the night.

With Olivia, a girl I only half knew and half trusted.

And she was about to take out my respirator. I blinked no, hoping she would see. I was awake now.

This wasn't a dream. This was a really bad idea.

"Don't worry, I've got this . . . I think." She smiled and moved to the side of the bed. "First, you have to turn off the alarm that will sound in the nurse's station when you're disconnected—I learned this one a long time ago." Her hand went to the side of the machine where she pressed a small button. "Override," she said in a singsong voice. She looked at the front of the respirator for a moment, studying the panel. "Now this part, I haven't done before. Here goes nothing." She turned the respirator off, then unhooked the tube quickly, bringing it around to the back of the chair. I could hear it click into place. "See? That was easy." She came back around to look at me. "You feel okay?" I blinked no, then no again. "What's wrong? I know it's in right." She looked over my shoulder at the machine under the chair. "Uh, why aren't you breathing?" Olivia looked frantic, checking the tube at my throat. Time seemed to slow down as I felt the last of my air escape my lungs, traveling down the tube, with nothing to replace it. I looked at Olivia but her face was like a mask, blank, unblinking. A crazy thought suddenly crossed my mind—Olivia was trying to hurt me. She wasn't happy for me, she didn't want me to get better. She wanted to keep me here, like her. Forever.

"West, West!" She looked into my face and opened my mouth with her fingers, bringing me back. "Oh shit!" She ran around the back of the chair. "Maybe there's something . . . ," she said, and turned on the portable respirator. I felt my lungs fill with air.

"Oh God." She came around the front of the chair and slumped onto the bed. "I forgot to turn it on! I almost killed you!" She started laughing hysterically, then caught herself and quieted down. "I thought this would be fun, a joyride, they made it look easy today when they took you out." She flopped back on the bed, looking exhausted, and let out a long sigh. Then she sat up quickly. "You are okay now, right? You feel okay?" I blinked yes. She seemed sincere. She just forgot to turn on the machine. She wasn't trying to hurt me. I didn't know why that thought crossed my mind. She wouldn't do that.

Olivia flopped down on the bed again and muttered, "Oh man, remind me never to get a job as a nurse."

It was weird to see her lying down while I was sitting up, her legs, long and white, hanging off the bed. Her thin hospital robe had fallen open and I could see that she was wearing a little pair of gym shorts and a tank top beneath it. Looking at her legs, something in my mind said "touch her," and I told my hand to move. I could almost feel her thigh under my hand, smooth and warm. But it didn't happen. My hand didn't move. For once I was happy not to be in control of my body. It kept me from doing something stupid with this beautiful girl.

She pulled herself up on her elbows on my bed and looked at me. "Well, I guess since I almost killed you, we should make the most of it, right?" I blinked yes, putting my thoughts about her body out of my mind, and she stood up, moving behind the chair. "Let's get this party started," she said, and pushed the chair out the doorway and quietly to the left—away from the nurses' station and toward the TV room. We had only gone by two or three rooms before we both heard something: footsteps. Moving quickly down the other hallway.

"Shhhhhh," Olivia whispered to me, and turned the wheelchair into the nearest open doorway. She backed the chair into the corner, just out of the view of the hallway light. At first, I thought the room was empty, but then as my eyes got used to the dark, I noticed that there was a ventilator running, lights blinking by the bed. There was someone there, quietly sleeping, a small thin person—maybe a woman or a kid. Olivia pushed the chair forward and peeked around the corner, watching until the nurse went by, on her way down the hall. "The coast is now clear," she said quietly, moving us out the doorway again. I wanted to know what was wrong with the person on the bed, why they were here, but there was no time to ask.

Olivia pushed me down the hallway, more quickly now, and took a sharp left into the TV room. I hadn't actually been in the room before, just wheeled by it. Now the TV was off, the room was dark and quiet. There was a table with some old boxed puzzles and board games piled on, some tattered magazines. It didn't look like many of the patients used this room. On the other wall, by the windows, was a computer—it was big and clunky. Olivia rolled me over in front of it, then went back and closed the door behind us.

"We probably shouldn't turn on the lights, but I don't think anyone will notice the door being closed. I've been in here at night before and the nurses didn't notice. They're always sitting at the desk, eating junk from the machine and reading magazines. No wonder they're all so chubby."

She reached behind the screen and turned it on. It had been a while since I'd seen my laptop; I missed it—I missed that connection to the world, to all my friends. I couldn't believe I'd gone so long without writing an e-mail or a text to anyone.

"The Internet in here sucks," Olivia said, typing in a few things. "Do you want to check your e-mail, or . . . ?" She shrugged. I did want to, but then I didn't. Who would have sent me an e-mail? Everyone had to know I was in the hospital. Like this. Even if anyone had sent me something, did I really want Olivia reading it over my shoulder? I blinked no.

"Okay." She pulled over a chair and sat next to me, taking a second to look at my face. "You're doing all right, though, the air is working and all that?" I blinked yes and she started typing on the keyboard. "Good. I have something to show you. Now, I'm only doing this because I owe you. You'll have something on me forever once you see this."

A website that hosted videos popped up on the screen and Olivia typed a few words into the search bar. After a moment, an image of a dance studio filled the screen, with five girls against a bar. "Oh yeah, jackpot." She pressed play and the girls started to move, dancing around the room. They each wore identical outfits: pale-pink leotards and tutus, pink tights and shoes. But one of them stood out. The palest girl, with black hair woven into a bun on top of her head. Her neck was long and straight, and even though I didn't know anything about ballet, I could tell she was the best in the group—her movements were effortless, exact.

"Yeah, that's me. Laugh it up." She looked at my face and could tell I wasn't laughing. That I was in awe of her. "Seems like another life." She pressed pause before I had seen enough and typed something else into the search bar. "You know what, I haven't even seen this one myself." An image of a large stage appeared on the screen and as the video started, you could hear clapping in the audience. Olivia turned down the volume, but I could still hear classical music begin as the curtain opened. Two rows of girls walked delicately down the stage and started to dance, spinning all in time, moving as one. I tried to pick Olivia out, but the camera was too far away; I couldn't tell one ballerina from another. Searching their faces and hair, I didn't see her. But then a lone dancer entered the stage from behind, all in white, a long flowing dress. Her hair was down, long and black, and it followed her as she twirled into place, right in the middle of the anonymous dancing girls.

She was stunning.

I glanced over at Olivia. Her face in the glow of the computer looked almost angry, like she hated that girl on screen, that gorgeous, talented girl. She caught my eye for a second and looked down. "I know what you're thinking, West, that's the beauty of this relationship. I can always tell what you're thinking, you don't even have to say it."

Her words were so familiar. Had she said this to me before?

"You're looking at her." She motioned to the screen, where the other Olivia was now joined by a guy dancer who was lifting her, gracefully, high over his head. "You're thinking, what happened to that girl? Where is she?" Olivia paused the screen on a shot of herself and the male dancer holding hands, looking into each other's eyes. "You know what, sometimes I wonder the same thing." Olivia stared at the screen for a moment, then her hand moved quickly to turn off the computer.

"That's the past; it's over." Her voice had no emotion. She turned her chair to face me. "This is now; this is where we're at. And if I weren't in here, I never would have met you. And you never would have met me. And I think we were supposed to meet. I don't know why, but we were." She looked so intense, she was scaring me a little. "Do you ever think about stuff like that?"

Her eyes locked on mine, so dark I couldn't decide if they were amazing or scary, but I blinked yes. "We were meant to know each other. I don't know why yet, but . . ." She took my hands in hers. "But we were." We sat like that for a few minutes, my hands in hers. She looked out the window at the almost full moon beyond, her dark hair down around her face. I could feel her hands in mine, just a little, just enough to tell they were small and delicate, but still strong. Like Olivia. She still was as beautiful as the girl on the screen, at least on the outside. But something had happened to Olivia on the inside, something terrible, to change her, to put her here. I could see that now. And I wondered if she would ever be able to tell me what it was.

Chapter 10

The room is dark, but Norris has left the curtains open for some reason, letting the cold moonlight pour in, making a rectangle on the floor. I see water, big drops, then a puddle. I trace it with my eyes until I see feet. A girl is standing in my room dripping on the floor. She's standing a few feet from my bed, staring at me.

"Olivia?"

"I didn't want to wake you."

"Why are you all wet?"

"I've been swimming." She's wearing her white night-gown, now soaked to transparent and sticking to her skin. I can see every curve of her body; her breasts are dark circles under the fabric.

"At the lake. I wanted you there, but I didn't want to wake you." She moves to the bed and takes my hand.

"You're ice," I tell her. "Get in." I move over and pull back the sheet. I know she'll be wet but I'm still startled at just how cold she is. Why did she go in a lake in the winter, at night, alone?

I feel like I know the answer and I shouldn't ask.

I lift the blanket over her body as she curls in against me and wrap my arms around her. She's thin, thinner than Allie; her body is unbelievably delicate, her hands are tiny. I curl around her tighter. I don't want to hurt her, but I feel like I can't hold her tight enough.

"That feels good," she says, and lets out a sigh.

———

"You are all cleaned up," the blond nurse said, rubbing a dry towel over my underarms. "Looking good, a new gown and we're ready." She pulled a new green-and-white patterned robe from her cart and slipped my arms into it, lifting me slightly on my side to snap the back. "And let's sit up a bit," she said, pushing a button on the side of the bed. She let the back of the bed come up behind my shoulders just a few inches. "Okay." She pushed my hair back to one side, then forward over my forehead, then over to the other side. "How do you do this?" I blinked twice for no, to tell her she didn't have to bother, but she didn't seem to know my code. I usually just let my hair do its own thing, but Mom liked it pushed back. "Well, that looks good," she finally said, letting it flop down like long bangs. She tidied up her cart and headed out of the room.

I didn't even want to think about the dream while the nurse was still in here, like I was afraid something on my face would give it away. That I had a sort of dirty dream. About Olivia. Did I like Olivia? Like, *really* like her? I lay there thinking about it, playing it over in my mind, how Olivia got into bed with me, how good it felt to curl up against her . . . until the real Olivia walked into the room.

"Heya, handsome, nice 'do," she joked. She pushed my hair back from my face the way it usually was and plopped down in the chair. It felt weird to have her touch my forehead, made me nervous. What if she could tell what I was thinking? Did she say that to me, or did I just dream it?

"So you must be tired this morning . . . I heard you were out late." She gave me an overly exaggerated wink.

As soon as Olivia said it, I remembered. We were out last night. Not for long, but we were. Went to the TV room, watched videos on the computer. She told me she knew what I was thinking, and she did. She held my hands. We watched her dancing.

"After you were back in bed, I couldn't sleep, so I thought I'd try to grab your files from the nurses' station— you know, just to see what this crazy doctor has in mind for you. But I couldn't get the goods. Every time I checked, there was someone there. The nurse who was on last night is lazy as hell and totally fell asleep at the desk. Usually there's a break when I can get in there."

The thought of Olivia sneaking to the nurses' station at night was funny, but it was also sad. I wondered if she had ever pulled her own file—and if she had read it, how it made her feel. She curled up in the chair, pulling her IV pole closer. "Don't look so stressed; I'm gonna try again tonight." She looked at my face a little closer, leaned in. "You okay? You don't look so good." She put her hand back on my forehead. "What the hell? You're burning up. What is wrong with these stupid nurses? I'll be right back." She yanked her IV pole behind her and stormed out of the room, muttering to herself.

In a few minutes, a nurse I'd never seen before came in. She checked my chart and adjusted something on the respirator, checked the tube going into my throat and adjusted my sheets. She looked at the monitor again and put her hand on my forehead. Then she made a face and marked something on the chart. After she left, I started to drift off. Being out for a midnight stroll really did wear me out; Olivia wasn't joking.

A guy in a white lab coat came into the room, and Nurse Norris was behind him. For some reason, the room seemed darker now, like the sun was going down. But it had just been morning.

"How long has his temperature been elevated?" the guy asked.

"About twenty-four hours, low-grade on and off."

"Hmmmm," the guy said. He looked at my chart and turned the page. "We want to avoid any type of infection. I see here that Dr. Louis is considering a vertebrate-fusion surgery on this patient. I'd like a full workup now, so that we aren't facing any infection-related delays later. And page me if his fever goes any higher."

"Of course, Doctor," Nurse Norris said. She walked out of the room with him and came back a moment later with a plastic cart full of medical stuff. "Got to take a little blood," she explained. It was dark out. What had happened to the day? Maybe those were storm clouds.

She straightened my arm and tied it off with a thick rubber band, wiping the inside of my elbow with an icy cold alcohol pad. "Little pinch," she said, sliding a needle into my arm. It did pinch and I flinched for a second, feeling like a baby. Nurse Norris met my eyes. "You felt that, didn't you?" she asked me. A huge smile crossed her face. "You sure did! I knew it, you're coming back all over." I realized that I had felt the alcohol wipe too, the chill of it. She pulled some blood from my arm into a tube and sealed it off, pulled out the needle, and put a small bandage over the spot. "When you first got here and I did your IVs, you didn't feel a thing. But now look," she said, laying a cool hand across my forehead.

I closed my eyes knowing that Norris would make everything right. In a minute, the dark-haired nurse was back, the mean one, and she had a doctor with her, a woman doctor. It was light in my room again, but I couldn't tell if it was the next day or the same day. "It could just be a simple virus, but we need to keep an eye on him and make sure that his lungs stay clear." She looked over at the monitor next to the bed and read the numbers. "One oh one; that's high, but it's not gotten any higher since last night. Ibuprofen every four hours, and I'd like the physical therapist in to tap his lungs, keep things nice and clear." The doctor wrote everything on the clipboard, then turned back a page or two. "Has Dr. Yung seen this workup?"

"I don't think so," she said, glancing over the doctor's shoulder. "He hasn't signed it, so I guess not."

"When he comes on shift tonight, can you have him take a look? I don't know what he was looking for, but I'm not seeing anything out of the ordinary here."

I loved hearing that. My blood was normal. At least one thing was working with this body.

"And who's next?" the doctor said, pulling a small pad out of her pocket. "Olivia Kemple, shunt infection . . . room 203?"

"That's right next door, I'll show you," the nurse said, leading her out. Shunt infection—right. That's what happens when you constantly pull your own IV out. Olivia Kemple, you are in trouble.

I tried to listen closely to hear what was going on in the

next room, but I just heard the doctor speaking very softly, I caught only a few words. Was that Olivia talking? Or the other nurse? It was useless, I couldn't hear enough to figure out how Olivia was going to work her way out of this one. I drifted off, feeling a little woozy, and when I woke up, it was daylight and I was lying on my side, looking out the window and someone was sort of pounding on the side of my rib cage—not hard, like a rhythmic massage. They went up one way and down the other way, hitting me with the side of a hand, in a chop-chop motion. "Okay, now we'll go to the other side, same thing." As she rolled me back over, I recognized the physical therapist from before, with the supershort blond hair. Kim. She moved around the other side of the bed and rolled me up on my left side, pulling my right arm in front of my body, then she started doing the same chop-chop motion up my side and down it again. After a little bit, it started to feel pretty good, like I could really get a deep breath every time the respiration pulled in. I tried to clear my throat; it felt like there was some stuff in there.

"Good job. Let's get that stuff out, you've just got a little cold," the therapist said. She rolled me onto my back again, so I was staring at the ceiling. She walked out of the room without even saying good-bye, but she was back in a minute or two with Nurse Norris. "His temp is still elevated today, but I think he's going to kick this without antibiotics. He's a strong young man—aren't you, Mr. West?" she said, leaning over me. "I'm going to pull all that stuff that Kim just loosened up out of there for you." She pulled on something by my throat, where the breathing tube went in, and I felt a pull of air, like when you take the hose out of the vacuum cleaner.

"Almost done," Norris said. "I'm going to suction your nose as well." She put the tube back into my throat and secured the big plastic halo around my neck and shoulders. With a small plastic nozzle, she put a tube up my nose and pulled out some gunk. I had to remember this next time I had a cold, it worked great. "Quick look in those ears," she said, reaching into her pocket for a small penlight. "Everything looks nice and clear in there, no infection. You just rest." She put her hand on my forehead again and held it there for a moment. When she stepped away, I realized the physical therapist had been in the room the whole time, watching, and she had this horrified look on her face. "Can he feel that?" she asked Norris.

"Of course!" She laughed. "He can feel everything, and I bet he feels a lot better now that we've loosened up those lungs a little. Time for him to rest, so let's go." Norris put her hand on Kim's back and guided her out of the room. I didn't get how Kim could have any sort of medical training and still think I was a vegetable or something.

Even though Norris had cleaned out what she could, I

still had that fuzzy head feeling you get with a bad cold. I wanted to cough, but when I tried to, the tube in my throat just got in the way so it was useless. I closed my eyes and waited for Olivia or my mom to come visit me. I wondered what the doctor said to Olivia, and how she explained the "problem" with her feeding tube. But mostly I just wanted Mom to come, to sit with me and go over my MRI and talk to me really plainly about what was next for me, and when I was going to get out of here. I closed my eyes. I would rest, get better, and we would move on to the next step. I was ready.

Chapter 11

The room is dark again; the curtains are open. I've been here before. I know there will be water on the floor, and there is. But those aren't Olivia's feet. They are sandals, small. It's a girl, standing at the foot of my bed, in a puddle of water. She's tiny and thin, her clothes dark and dripping wet, her hands down by her side.

"Who are you?" She doesn't move, doesn't answer. "Can I help you?"

She moves closer to the side of the bed, to the drawer there. She reaches out her hand to open it and I can hear her sniffling; she's crying. I see a drop of water fall from her hand onto the floor. But it's not water; it's too dark, black. I trace it back up to her fingers.

It's blood. A cloud moves slowly away from the moon,

and more light pours into the room. I can see now that she's dripping blood, a puddle of it, streaked across the floor where she walked to the bed. She looks into the drawer, searching for something, but then suddenly her head turns and she sees that I'm there, that I'm awake—her hand shoots out from the drawer to my wrist, fast—she grips tight, tighter. It feels like she's trying to break my arm, her hand is ice, so cold it feels like it's burning my skin. "Let go, stop," I tell her, but I can't pull away. I can't move. Her eyes are black circles. "Nurse!" I yell. "NURSE!"

"Nurse!" It wasn't my voice, it was my mom's.

"I heard you," the mean nurse said, rounding the corner of the doorway into the room.

"He's burning up—something is not right!" Mom yelled. "Look at his heart rate! What kind of hospital is this!"

"Mrs. Spencer, please calm down," the nurse said. "He has an elevated temperature, but we're doing everything we can to keep him comfortable."

"It's not enough—he's sick, something's wrong." Mom's hands gripped the rail at the side of my bed. "He's unresponsive."

The nurse took her penlight from her pocket and flashed it into my right eye quickly, back and forth. "He's not unresponsive; he's okay. Please have a seat and I'll send the doctor in to talk to you." She walked out of the room shaking her head.

Mom took my hand. "Hold on baby, hold on. I'm going to get you some help." I wasn't feeling that bad; in fact, I was feeling a little bit better than I had before I'd fallen asleep.

"Mrs. Spencer?" A tall, dark-haired doctor I'd seen once or twice came into the room. "I'm Dr. Yung. You have some concerns about your son's condition?"

"He's got this fever; I can see it on the monitor. It's at one hundred and one right now, and he's been like this for three days. When I was talking to him just now, his eyes rolled back in his head. He looked like he was having a seizure."

The doctor nodded. "That's not uncommon in his state—he might twitch, jerk uncontrollably. Rolling his eyes is just another one of those ticks that he's not in full control of yet."

"I've never seen him do that before; are you sure he's okay? He's never run a fever for this long."

"His body has been through a lot of trauma, and he's trying to heal. If you add a virus on top of that, you can see how his immune system is not what it was before the accident. It's harder for him to evacuate mucus from his lungs and to fight a fever. Unfortunately, what would be a cold for someone else is more like a lung infection for him, pneumonia. It is serious, but I can assure you, he's not in any discomfort, and we're keeping a close eye on him."

Mom sat down in the chair next to the bed. "I just don't know how much more of this I can take." She started crying. "I just don't know what to do."

The doctor pulled up the other chair and sat next to her. "Some of this you have to leave to us and know that we are taking the very best care of your son. If you're talking about his options for the future, those are decisions that you and West's father will have to make, and I understand it can be difficult."

Mom grabbed a tissue and wiped her nose. "We've been doing a lot of research, and I think we've made a decision, but the odds are so hard to face. I hope we're doing the right thing."

The doctor reached over and held Mom's hand. "Remember, he is very young, so the potential risks that you have been reading about are much lower for him. Once he kicks this virus, you can schedule the procedure at any time. He's stable and ready for the next step."

Mom nodded silently.

The doctor stood up. "Let me know if there's anything else I can do for you, Mrs. Spencer. Remember that we all want what's best for West, we really do."

Mom nodded again, taking another tissue. She blew her nose once he was out the door. She took my hand and held it for a few minutes quietly.

"West, honey, I need to talk to you." She stood up and leaned over me. "The procedure that Dr. Louis says you need is risky; there's a ten percent chance you won't make it. That means out of one hundred patients who have this, ten will die. Ten. I don't know if I can face those odds. But I also feel like you deserve the chance to have a normal life again. Tell me what you want to do." She stared into my eyes. I blinked once for yes, without a moment of hesitation.

Mom kept looking at me. Maybe she needed to be sure, so I blinked again. A smile crossed her face and she pushed my bangs back. "Do you remember Henry's birthday party at the pool—you all were six or seven. You took one look at that high dive and went right over to the ladder. You climbed without looking back and stood way out on the board. You looked at me for a second, then jumped off. I was so afraid, the other moms too. But you weren't. You never were." She kissed my forehead. "I know what you want to do; I know how strong you are," she whispered.

She sat back down and held my hand again. I was glad she had finally told me everything. And I could tell her how I felt. I squeezed her hand back and we sat like that, in silence, just listening to the whooshing sounds of the respirator, until I fell asleep.

Chapter 12

I woke up hearing music. Loud, hip-hop. My favorite CD from last fall, a band called Water Gun. The room was bright, sunny, and sitting next to me, an iPod speaker system blasting. The speakers were covered in stickers from a burger joint, the kind they usually give to little kids. I had seen those speakers before . . . Mike. That was Mike's system. I looked around the room. Mike's back was to me, but it was him, there was no mistaking his crazy curly red hair in knots, almost like dreadlocks. He was jamming out at the foot of my bed. He spun around on one foot. "Dude, do you remember when they did this song at the Music Box, and that girl totally jumped up on stage. I think she got kicked out." He was trying to do some moves like the guys do in the video, but failing so badly it made me want to close my eyes again. Mike was awesome on the bike, but as a dancer, his moves were laughable. "She was hot, though. I wouldn't have kicked her out."

Nurse Norris poked her head into the room. "I'm sorry, but you're going to have to turn that down."

"Wha, I can't hear you," Mike joked, cupping his hand to his ear.

She walked in and turned the volume down herself. "I told you last time you were here. Music is okay, but it's not a dance party. This is a hospital." She gave him a stern look and turned to walk out.

"Really, did one of the other patients complain? I mean, I'm just wondering." This attitude was exactly why Mike had been getting detention on a regular basis since ninth grade.

Norris let out a sigh. "Even if the patients didn't complain, their families and other visitors might. You can play music, just keep it down. Clear?"

"Crystal," Mike said, trying to pop-lock but instead looking like a total idiot. I was surprised he didn't fall down.

Norris scowled and left the room. I know she had a smile on her face the second she turned the corner; how could she not laugh at Mike's so-called dancing?

"Man, the nurses here suck. They aren't even hot." Mike plopped into the chair next to the bed and leaned in to turn up the volume one or two clicks. "Whatever."

Mike always told you exactly how he felt; sometimes that was great, sometimes it sucked. The first day I met him, I was at the bike park. I'd seen him there before, but we went to different schools, so we didn't talk. Then, right before ninth grade started, he walked over to me. "You got hella tall, man," he said, looking me up and down.

"Uh, yeah, I guess I did," I said back. I didn't know if it was okay to say that I'd noticed his crazy red hair and incredible skills on the track, so I just kept my mouth shut.

"Yeah, you were, like, a shrimp before. What happened?"

"I dunno. My dad is tall," I offered. Mike stood there staring at me; he wanted more of an explanation. He wasn't put together badly; he had broad shoulders and weighed at least ten pounds more than me, but he was also about half a foot shorter, sort of a stocky build.

"Actually, it kind of hurt," I confessed. "I woke up during the night all winter. My bones, like, hurt."

"Seriously?" He was loving it. "Hurt how?"

"It's hard to explain, but my muscles would hurt in the morning. And at night I would get these pains, like cramps in my legs and stuff. That happened for months. It really sucked."

"But now you're supertall. Are you going to keep growing?" he asked.

I shrugged. "No idea. My dad is six-two, so maybe."

"Damn." Mike scraped some mud off his bike shoe.

He told me that there had been some girls from my school looking for me at the track, the day before. "Not ugly," he pointed out. I had no idea who they could be, but I knew what was probably going on. Eighth grade was a big one for me: I grew half a foot, got my braces off, and started wearing contacts more—mostly because my glasses got in the way with my helmet. I looked different, and it seemed like the girls at school had noticed and decided I was cute, or something. A group of them started acting weird around me, giggling all the time, saying stupid stuff to me.

The next day at the track, Mike was there again and pointed out the girls sitting on a bench. They were from my English class and obviously there to see me; they waved enthusiastically the second I looked their way. "Hook me up," Mike said, parking his bike next to mine. "The blonde is awesome." So we walked with the girls to Mel's Pizza and grabbed some slices, Mike doing his best to make conversation with the blond girl while I was stuck talking to the other one. She wasn't ugly, but she had on too much makeup and lip stuff and was wearing high heels, which seemed weird to me. She could barely walk. All she wanted to talk about were other girls from our school: who was cool, who wasn't. "Do you know Candace? She's so pretty. Oh, do you know Ariel? She's okay. Do you know Amy?

I hate her." It went on like this the whole time. I couldn't get out of there fast enough. But Mike had a great time and was into the blond girl. I got the impression he didn't get to hang out with girls very much; he acted like a spaz the entire time. The girl seemed a little into it; she laughed at some of his jokes, but in the end, she didn't give him her number. As we biked back, Mike flipped up his visor at a stop sign and turned to me. "My man, I can't thank you enough. From here on out, I'm your wingman whenever you need one." He reached out to shake my hand and gripped hard.

It turned out that we were both starting at Marshall High that fall, and Mike made sure my transition to ninth grade was smooth. He knew a lot of the upperclassmen, so instead of getting harassed and hazed like some of the other ninth-grade scrubs, we were in with the populars from day one: had a cool lunch table to sit at, knew which teachers to avoid, where to hang out, whose classes you could skip, everything. Mike thought I brought girls around, that he was my wingman, but really, he was the one who took me from nerd to popular overnight. I owed him everything— including Allie. But I'd never told him.

I glanced over at him sitting next to the hospital bed and felt a wave of emotion. When I got out of here, I was going to tell him how much I appreciated his friendship, even if he thought that was cheesy. I wanted him to know.

He took a swig from his soda and nodded his head to the music. "This is riding-around-in-Malcolm's-car music, right? Remember when we all went on that beer run that night, when it was snowing? I could feel the bass line through my sneakers." He took another drink and sat staring out the window for a moment. "You did that hilarious impression of Mr. Perkins. 'Stu-DENTS, now, stu-DENTS!' Damn, I thought I was going to pee my pants." He laughed at the memory. My impression of our principal always made Mike laugh. But his face didn't look too happy right now. "I miss that stuff. Just the stupid stuff, ya know? That was a fun night," he added quietly. He looked a little uncomfortable with the silence that fell over the room when the song ended. He pushed a button on the iPod and started another song by a different band. "Anyways, ancient history, right?" He stood and walked around the bed, his restless energy making me nervous. "You have to fill me in on when the hot nurses are working because every time I'm here it's Ugly and Uglier."

I didn't remember Mike ever being here before; it must have been before I woke up. And I didn't like him calling Norris ugly. She wasn't a sexy porno nurse, but she was an awesome lady. I liked her.

"Maybe some hot lady patients, huh? Have you been checking them out? I know you have." I instantly thought of Olivia and felt my face turn red. I hoped Mike didn't notice. How long had it been since I hung out with Olivia anyhow? I knew I'd been sick and a day or two had gone by. Maybe more? I hadn't really seen her since the dream where she climbed into bed with me. I didn't want to think about that, especially not with Mike here. Made me feel like I was cheating on Allie. I had to remind myself that we weren't really together anymore, so it wouldn't be cheating. Even if it did happen, which it didn't, because it was just a dream. But we did hold hands that night, in the TV room. Something had happened there. Something she said. I tried to clear my foggy head and pay attention to Mike, but he was talking so fast and all over the place, he was making my head spin. Had he always been this hyper?

"Did I already tell you about Erin, the new girl? I think I did, but I'm gonna tell you again. Her face is just okay, so don't be surprised when you see her. She's no Allie, ya know? But the body. Ohmigod, the body. It's like *Sports Illustrated*. Of course Perry the Perv is all over her. Already asked her out like ten times. She wore this skirt . . ." He motioned to mid-thigh to show me how short it was, then shook his head and closed his eyes, as if to wash away the image before he could go on talking. "Anyway, I'm just waiting for the right time to swoop down and ask the lady out. Maybe we can double date, me and Erin and you and Allie, when you get out of here. Think about it, okay?"

Allie obviously hadn't told him that she dumped me.

I couldn't deal with getting into it all, so I blinked once for yes, and Mike quickly moved his eyes from mine. It felt like he didn't want to spend too long looking at my face, like I grossed him out or something. "Cool, okay." He nodded in time to the music. He stared out the window again and looked lost in thought; it was as if he had forgotten I was there. Something gave me the impression he didn't like it here—and that he wouldn't be back anytime soon.

Norris came into the room and picked up my chart at the foot of the bed. "As much as West loves having you here, I'm afraid visiting hours are almost up," she told Mike.

"Not a problem; we were pretty much done," he said. He unplugged the speaker and grabbed it by the handle on top. He stood up and saluted me like a soldier in the army. "West, my brother, be well. See you soon." He did an elaborate bow to Nurse Norris, with a hand flourish at the end. "Lady Nurse, I bid you adieu," he told her, turned on his heel, and walked out.

Norris moved to the side of the bed to take my pulse. "That boy is crazy." She smiled. "But I can tell his heart is in the right place. You, on the other hand, are doing so much better today. A week of fever and finally you are on the mend. Pneumonia is no fun, huh?"

Could it have been a week? I must have really been out

of it. Felt like just a day or two. I wondered what was up with Olivia; where had she been? Then I had a horrible feeling. What if something had happened to her? If she was sick too? She was really thin; if she got pneumonia, it could kill her. Or what if her mom transferred her to another hospital? I suddenly remembered the dream: a little girl in sandals, dripping blood, looking for something in that drawer. The dream was trying to tell me something: Olivia was sick, or gone. The thought of not seeing her made my chest hurt, like someone had just put a giant brick on top of my body.

I stared at the clock and wished Olivia would open the wall and walk in. Maybe I could send her a subconscious message or something. She said she knew my thoughts. But it didn't seem to work. Instead I just lay there feeling miserable until Mom showed up around six. "So happy you are feeling better!" she said brightly. "Look at you! I can just tell looking at your face that you are on the mend." She pulled a chair over to the bed and held my hand. "So tomorrow, you can get back into the wheelchair, and I can even take you on a walk. Won't that be exciting?"

It didn't really sound that great to me, so I blinked no, but Mom went right on. "And I'm sure you're curious about your surgery. Dr. Louis has been updated on how you've been doing, and he just needs to see your blood work before we schedule anything. He said maybe in a week or two, okay? Once we get your white blood cell count back down to normal, and that shouldn't take long."

A week or two sounded like forever; I'd already been in here a month. I wanted my old life back. I was ready to do this now, not in two weeks.

"Well, since we finished *Harry Potter*, I picked up that book Allie said your class was reading." Mom reached into her bag and pulled out a paperback. Just the thought of Allie, of reading the same thing she was reading, made me feel terrible. I didn't want to think about her, about school, about English class, my old friends, my old life. I didn't even remember Mom finishing *Harry Potter*.

Allie dumped me. Mike couldn't even look at me. The one person who actually seemed to get it had suddenly disappeared. Where was Olivia? Why hadn't I seen her for days? She said she needed a friend, and I thought I was one. Guess I was wrong. My world had gotten really small, and it felt like it was getting smaller.

"Oh, your eyes are still so watery." Mom leaned over me with a tissue and cleaned up my face. She assumed it was just from being sick that my eyes were watering, and I was glad for the excuse.

Mom started to read *A Separate Peace*, about an older guy who goes back to visit where he went to high school. He's walking around remembering things that happened to him, and I could just tell this guy had a sad story to tell—something bad was going to happen to somebody, and I didn't want to hear it. I tuned out the words Mom was reading. Two more weeks, that's the goal. I had to focus on that, on getting out of here, on the surgery being successful. Two more weeks.

Chapter 13

West, wake up." I heard a girl's voice talking to me. "West." Her hand was on my arm, just like in the dream, the little girl covered in blood.

"It's just me," Olivia said when I started. She was sitting on the side of my bed. "Are you better? I was worried about you."

I blinked yes and she was visibly relieved. "I got a little busted myself." She motioned to her feeding tube. "Infection. I guess a lady should wash her hands before pulling out an IV tube on a regular basis, huh?" She smiled and I felt something in my chest let go. Olivia was still here. She was okay.

"I wanted to come by, but they were checking you a lot, plus you were sort of out of it. But I was thinking about you." She sounded so serious, like a greeting card. "I couldn't help thinking about you, especially when I was trying to read tonight and your friend was here blasting rap music." She scowled at me. I was happy to have the sarcastic Olivia back.

"So." She took a deep breath. "While you were busy being sick, I was busy being Harriet the Spy. Finally got a nurse on night duty who liked to smoke—a lot—so I had some time at the nurses' station to do a little research."

She scooted over on the bed, closer to me, and pushed the button to raise it up, so I was sitting looking at her. "Here's the thing: I'm not sure you're going to like what I found out." She leaned in to me as she whispered. "Number one, I looked up the guy who was in this room before you, not a pretty picture. Remember how you told me you're having bad dreams about a man?"

I blinked yes and she went on.

"Was he—I know this sounds gross—but was he, like, burned?"

No.

"Are you sure he wasn't burned in a fire, or on fire or anything in your dream?"

Again I had to blink no. I had no idea where she was going with this.

"Hmmmmm." This was obviously not what she wanted to hear. "The guy who was here before you, he was burned really badly—that's why he was in a coma. It was a medically induced coma; they were trying to fix his skin with grafts and stuff. But I guess he got a bad infection. . . ." She trailed off. "Anyhow, it was gross reading his medical file. I just thought maybe you were dreaming about him, about that, about a fire or a burned guy?"

I blinked no. I could tell Olivia was disappointed. She thought she had a ghost story on her hands, and that she had solved it, and here I was letting her down. But then I started thinking, what if this guy had done something terrible to someone—what if that's why he was burned? What if he attacked that girl, and then . . . who knows? Her boyfriend or her dad came and did something terrible to him, burned him? I motioned with my eyes to the drawer where Olivia kept the whiteboard.

"Oh, sorry, of course, I'm having a one-sided conversation here." She pulled out the board and slipped the pen into my hand. I wrote *How.*

"How what?" Olivia said. "How did I find out? I looked up his records in the office. Trust me, it wasn't easy. The nurse—"

I motioned to the board again and Olivia stopped talking and placed it by my hand. *Burn,* I wrote.

"*How. Burn.* How was he burned? I don't know, it didn't say . . . or maybe I didn't look close enough. Should I try to find out? You think this is connected somehow?"

I blinked yes. It had to be. It made no sense that I would be having these violent dreams about this guy; there had to be a connection.

I looked at the board again, and Olivia wiped it off for me. *Photo*, I wrote this time.

"You're a genius," she said, smiling and touching my shoulder. "There were pictures in his file, pretty gruesome stuff, but I'll get you one. If you recognize him . . ." She shivered visibly. "Creepy, right?"

I blinked yes. She was on to something, I could feel it.

Olivia sighed and closed her eyes for a second, like she was thinking. "There's something else. While I was in the office, I looked at your file, too." She paused, her face revealing nothing. "Do you want to know?" I blinked yes, and she went on.

"It's not good news, I'm warning you," she said sadly, taking the pen from my hand and holding my fingers in hers. "It looks like this doctor, Dr. Louis, wants to do this experimental surgery on you, but . . ."

I waited for her to tell me the stuff I already knew: it was risky, my mom didn't want to do it, I had to wait two weeks, what?

"No one seems to think it will work. According to the files, he's done it on only a few patients, and I guess it hasn't gone that well." She looked down at my hand, like she was inspecting my fingers. "I guess a few people have died, too."

When she looked up, I could tell she was genuinely sad for me. "I'm sorry."

This wasn't really news to me; I had gotten the feeling from Mom's attitude that this wasn't a hundred percent chance at recovery for me, but I guess I also hadn't known my chances were so bad.

"I only had about two minutes to look at both files, but from what I saw in yours, the doctors here think you should go a more natural route, see what sensation comes back on its own, try getting by with the wheelchair for now. They think the surgery is radical, and the risks aren't worth it."

I looked to the board and she put the pen back in my hand. I wrote one word: *You.*

Olivia took in a deep breath. "What do I think?" she asked, and I blinked yes. "I don't know, to be honest with you, about the medical care here, about the doctors. Heck, I don't trust *any* doctors anymore, I've been in hospitals for so long." She sighed. "I mean, is it so terrible to wait a month or two and see what happens? You haven't been here that long." She looked at me with a small smile. "If you wait a few months and you're still like this, have the surgery. But what if they're right, and things come back on their own?" I thought of how I felt the needle the last time Norris drew my blood, felt the cold sting of the alcohol wipe. It was coming back, but how much would return, and how quickly? And what if it didn't?

She leaned in and pushed my hair back from my forehead, like Mom always did. For a second it seemed like she was going to kiss me, and the dream about her in bed with me flashed through my mind. Why was Olivia suddenly being so sweet to me? What had she seen in the file that made her feel so damn sorry for me? It was weird for her to come and see me at night, to sit on my bed instead of in a chair. Maybe the odds were worse than Mom told me; maybe there was a chance I would have the surgery and still be like this, stuck like this forever. No one had talked about that.

My paranoia began to set in, and it was as if she could feel me growing cold to her. "You know, I almost didn't tell you this, but . . . if the tables were turned, if you knew something like this about me, I would want to know." She paused to meet my eyes. "So I decided to tell you. You're the only person who really gets it in here, so we've got to look out for each other." Her words echoed in my head. Hadn't I just been thinking the same thing a few hours ago, that Olivia was the one person who got it? It was a glimmer of hope that she felt the same way about me.

Olivia leaned in to me, laying her head on my chest. "I can hear your heart beating," she whispered, putting her arms around me. She snuggled in and let out a sigh, curling her body next to mine.

Allie always smelled a little like strawberries, like

outdoors. She told me it was just her shampoo, but she smelled like summer to me. Olivia was different. She wasn't like a high-school girl. The way she moved her body close to mine made me feel I was grown up. She smelled like perfume, like a woman would wear, something musky and rich. I heard her breathing grow more quiet and regular and realized that she had fallen asleep, holding me, her long hair falling softly over my chest and onto the white sheets.

Chapter 14

There's blood on my hands. It's up to my wrists, splattered on my arms. I look all over my legs, my stomach, my shirt, my pants. Where's the cut? I can't find it. It's so much blood. I open my palms and see that the blood has dried into the creases, the lines of my fingers; in places it's turning dark brown. But I'm not bleeding. I have no pain. It's not my blood. I hear sirens in the distance and know I have to run. They can't catch me. Running feels so good. I'm so powerful, there's no way that they can catch me. I'm too smart for them. I'm moving like I have superpowers, off the sidewalk now and through a yard, over a stone wall in one leap, through the back of a parking lot. I'm down behind a car, breathing hard when I see myself, a reflection in the car's windows. Something isn't right, my hair is black.

I move to the side mirror on the car. It's dark out, but the security light from the parking lot is bright enough to see my face in the mirror. It isn't my face, it's his face. I'm him. I'm him.

———

I was finally wide awake. After so many hazy days, so many drugs and half-awake moments, I was completely awake, aware. I could feel the roughness of the sheets under my skin, hear and sense everything, the sound of the machines next to me. How could I ever sleep with that sound going on? My mind was racing, realizing that I hadn't seen my face since the accident that put me here. I was still me, wasn't I? Who was I? I was West. West Spencer. Junior at Marshall High School. I have blond hair, green eyes. Hazel eyes according to my girlfriend. My ex-girlfriend. That was all real.

But what if it wasn't real.

Did I have black hair and brown eyes—was I covered in someone else's blood? Had I done something terrible that no one could tell me about, that I couldn't even admit to myself? What if this was a mental institution and I was completely insane? Could I have created a whole new personality? I had to see a mirror to be sure I was who I thought I was. Olivia could get me one. Because Olivia was real. She was just here with me. She must have gotten up and gone back to her room, before the nurse checks.

I focused back on visits from my mom, my dad, the doctors, nurses, Olivia, Mike, Allie. She broke my heart. That happened. I'm not imagining it. And Olivia, falling asleep with me, holding me. The way that felt. That was real. I just had a dream, a dream that I was actually someone else. But that's not me. I didn't do anything to anyone. I didn't hurt anyone. That person, that man with dark hair, he is not me. I need to see a photo of the man who was in this room before me, and a mirror. But I know already: he is not me. I'm not him. Unless . . . but no.

I didn't do anything. I would remember.

I was in an accident, at the bike course, on the ramp at the quarry. I know that happened. I tried to replay it in my mind, and it was foggy, but it happened. It did.

I tried to change the images in my head: the dark-haired guy, his bloody hands, that feeling of being so powerful and strong and invincible. It was a great feeling, like the way I felt on the bike when everything was going great, the way I felt when I was in my first race and knew I was going to place. I wanted that feeling, I craved it, I wanted to have it again. Like the night I met Allie and I knew she liked me back. The way I felt when Olivia was in my room last night, when I hadn't seen her in a few days, how good it felt to just look at her face, how my heart started to beat and I felt alive. Everyone wants to feel that way. But not with bloody hands, not as someone else. Maybe I was just having this dream because I missed feeling alive. Maybe it has nothing to do with that guy, or with the guy who stayed in this room before me. But I had a nagging feeling in my gut that it was connected, somehow.

Something was just not right, like Olivia said: my dreams were trying to tell me something. I had to figure out what it was. Something about this hospital, this room. Something key. And I wasn't going to be able to shake this feeling until I figured it out—until we figured it out.

I glanced at the clock. Four in the morning. Hours before Olivia would be awake. Hours before anyone would be in here to see me, to see that I was awake. I practiced moving my hands, like I'd been doing lately when I found myself awake but with no visitors, not drugged up, nothing to do. I moved the fingers on my right hand, trying to make a fist. I was almost there. The fingers on my left hand were not as strong. I could close them a little, enough to fit around a bike handle, but not enough to hold on tightly. And it was hard. I had to focus entirely on it. I went back to the right hand and tried to close it three times, then on to the left. I had to show the physical therapist the next time she was back—the one who thought I was a vegetable—show her what I could do.

I fell asleep clenching my right hand tight enough to feel my nails digging into my palm, letting go only when I felt a soft hand touch mine. Olivia. "Hey, you could feel that?" she asked, her dark eyes growing larger. "You felt me touch your hand; you moved. You are coming around, the doctors were right." The sun was up, my room was washed in light. I couldn't even see the clock, but it must have been midmorning. I noticed Olivia didn't have her IV stand with her as she pulled a chair closer to the bed. She had the same look on her face that she did when she learned that I was going to be able to be in a wheelchair—happy for me, but not really. A little bit worried, too.

"Well, if you're getting all grabby, I should be a little more careful, huh? You know you almost got me in trouble last night." She gave me a sideways look, obviously a little embarrassed. "And I thought I could trust a paralyzed boy—I thought you loved me for my mind." She flipped her long hair over her shoulder, then laughed. "Seriously, we did almost get so busted. I woke up about two seconds before Norris did her checks. Can you imagine?" It was good to see a big smile on her face, to hear her laugh for real. "I would have had some explaining to do!"

She took my hand and looked at my face, getting quiet for a moment. "You're thinking hard about something, what is it?" I moved my eyes to the drawer.

"You want to write something?" She took the board out and raised the back of my bed up slightly. She put the pen into my right hand and I grasped it quickly. "My favorite student, you have been practicing!"

I felt my chest expand with pride. Of course she was the first person to notice. She held the board up for me and I wrote one word.

"Mirror? You . . . want to see a mirror? For yourself?" Olivia let out a little laugh. "What, I sleep over with you one time and you want to check yourself out, see if you still got it?"

I blinked no, but she was having too much fun to stop. "I should have known. All you good-looking guys are all the same. You want to fix your hair just right, make sure you're still hot . . . okay, I get it. I'll be right back, pretty boy." Olivia shook her head as she opened the room divider, but then she turned around. "Actually, I think I saw . . ." She moved around the bed to the small table and opened the drawer. Watching her look inside made me feel sick with déjà vu. A little girl looking in the drawer for something. Crying, dripping blood. Was that something that really happened?

"Here we go, handsome." Olivia was holding up a mirror with a short plastic handle. She held it tightly to her chest, so I couldn't see it. "Are you ready to see how gruesome you've become?" she joked, then turned the mirror around, close to my face.

I was me. Same hair, but longer. Too long. And it looked dirty, like I hadn't washed it in a week. I tried to remember when was the last time a nurse washed my hair, but I couldn't. My eyes were still hazel-green. I had a little stubble on my face, just a little. I only had to shave about once every couple of weeks, so that was new for me. I looked older. Sort of better, actually. I could see the respirator tube, connected to a big white plastic neck brace. I was glad you couldn't actually see it going into my throat, or where the hole was. The tube just disappeared into the neck brace. It looked like something the football players wore under their uniforms. It wasn't as bad as I thought it would be.

"Do you need more time—I mean, should I leave you alone with your pretty self?" Olivia joked. "Just let me know if you need some privacy."

I blinked no and she took the mirror down; now I was just looking at her face. I was happy to be right, to be me. Olivia smiled and pushed my hair back. "Did you like what you saw?" She wasn't joking now; actually, she looked a little concerned.

I didn't want to blink yes or no. I did like what I saw, because it was me and not someone else, someone who did terrible things. But I didn't like how I looked now—with long greasy hair and stubble growing in patches all over my face—for Olivia's sake. I wanted her to see me the way the girls at school saw me, put together and clean. Wearing jeans, not a hospital robe. I wanted her to see me like that.

"You're a great-looking guy, West. You must know that." Olivia put the mirror back into the drawer and slid it shut.

"I know the girls at your school must go crazy for you." Again she had read my thoughts. She slipped her hand into mine and looked out the window. "I can see it too, don't get me wrong." She looked back at my eyes. "Yeah, you're hot," she said reluctantly. "But . . . getting to know you here," she said, and let go of my hand and motioned to the room around us. "It's not about that, it's about this." She put her hand on my chest and held it there. "Even if your pretty face had been messed up in the accident, I wouldn't care. You're still you." She moved her hand up to my cheek and sat looking at me for a long time. I couldn't help but think of what was going unsaid. That even though I couldn't walk, I was still me. That even if the surgery didn't work, I was still West. And somehow, Olivia had gotten to know me, in spite of all that. And she liked who I was. She liked me, the way I was now.

"The things that happened to us, to both of us, changed who we are, but—" She stopped herself. "Maybe we're not that different from how we used to be, right?"

I looked at the board and she understood I wanted to write something. She reached over to hold it up. It was a long word, so it took me a second. I wrote the word *beautiful*. Olivia took the board and held it in her lap, looking at it. Then she leaned across me, putting her lips on mine, kissing me, softly at first, gently, then hard and fast, her hands on my face, and in my hair. No one had touched me so roughly, so close since the accident. She stopped just as quickly as she had started, leaning in to me and whispering my name in my ear. "West . . ." She sat back and looked at me. "Your mom is coming to take you for a walk today; it's Saturday." She jumped up and straightened her robe, glancing at the clock. She stopped for a second, picked up the board, and read the word again to herself.

"I'm going to take this with me, if you don't mind." She smiled and hugged the board to her chest as she walked around the foot of my bed, to the divider wall. "But I'll see you later." She gave me one last glance as she slid the door shut and I heard her let out a little laugh, like this was crazy, insane. And she was right. It was crazy. What was going on? Olivia was into me. And I was falling for her. I was in the hospital, paralyzed, and crushing on the most unusual, confusing, beautiful, mysterious, amazing girl I'd ever met.

Chapter 15

Hey, look at you!" Mom walked in about half an hour after Olivia left. "You look great today!" I had been thinking about Olivia, so it must have been all over my face. I was never very good at hiding my feelings.

"So today is a big day; I'm taking you for a walk. Outside!" Mom was so thrilled, she was practically clapping. Even though she could be annoyingly enthusiastic sometimes, I was pretty psyched to see her so happy. Her past couple of visits had not been the best. "And as soon as we get you into your chair"—she glanced up at the clock—"I have got such a surprise for you. Really huge."

The male aide with red hair walked into the room behind her. "Are you ready?"

"Oh, we are ready," Mom answered excitedly. He moved

to the side of the bed to raise me up higher, then dropped the bed so my legs would hang down.

"We like to have them sit up for a couple of minutes before they go in the chair, just to get the blood going," he explained. He went to get my wheelchair from the corner of the room and set it up next to the bed. "I'll be right back."

"Isn't he handsome," Mom murmured. "Reminds me of Mike a little. Or what Mike could look like if he cut that hair. Speaking of." She moved closer to me and brushed my long bangs back. "What are we going to do about this? I wonder if they have a nurse here who can cut it, or if I should bring someone in. . . ."

The aide walked back in behind her and moved over to the bed.

"Are you going to do this all by yourself?" Mom asked nervously.

"It's easier than you think. Actually, you could do it. We'll teach you how to transfer him before he goes home," the guy explained.

"Oh no, he's not going home with a wheelchair—he's going to have surgery next week. We're hoping for the best!" She crossed her fingers and gave the guy a big smile.

"Is that so," he said, raising his eyebrows. He didn't look too convinced as he leaned in to me and put his arm around my back, much like Olivia had done but with a little more strength and the smoothness that comes with practice. He tilted me over his back and transferred me into the chair in about two seconds, snapping the armrests up and moving over the IV bag. "This is always the last step," he explained to Mom, turning off my respirator, then reattaching the tube to the back of the chair. He flipped the switch and I heard the portable turn on, pumping air into my lungs. "That's it—just in case you ever need to know," he said.

"Oh, I don't think I will," she said, but Mom's face looked nervous, like she was unsure herself as she watched him slip my feet into the footrests.

"He's ready to go. This is the brake." He showed Mom the pedal as she stepped behind the chair. "Any questions?" When Mom shook her head, he turned to leave. "We're around if you need anything." I was glad to see him go. Something about the guy was annoying, patronizing, like he didn't think Mom could push me in a wheelchair, or that I was never getting out of here. He was a dick.

"He sure made that look easy," Mom said to herself as she pushed me slowly through the door. "Let's head down to the nurses' station real quick." Mom pushed the chair to the right and I could see the low counter where the nurses hung out—a few computers and lots of paperwork scattered around. "Hi," she said brightly to the nurses on duty. "We are expecting a few visitors today and I just wanted you to know that we'll be . . . oh, look, here they come!"

Through the double doors at the end of the hall, I could

see three people walking in: one was Mike, his red hair impossible to hide. Another was my dad, tall and thin; I would know him anywhere. The third person was a little girl in a long black coat; it took me a second to realize that it was Allie—my Allie, with her hair all tucked under a hat. When they got inside, she took her hat off and shook her blond hair out, none of them realizing that I was sitting just a few feet away until Mom called out.

"Hey, there, guess who!"

"Oh man, it is good to see you." Dad made long strides and reached me first. I could see tears in his eyes, or maybe it was just really cold out and his eyes were watery. He knelt in front of the chair and put his hands on mine. "You look good—last time I saw you, you were not feeling so hot; you had a high fever, but wow. . . . Would you look at him?" Dad stood quickly and turned to Mom and gave her a big hug. "He looks good, he looks great, right?"

Mom was standing behind me so I couldn't see her, but I could hear that she was sniffling. I turned my attention to Mike and Allie. "How's it hanging?" Mike reached over and gave me a half fist-bump on my knuckles, then stood there awkwardly looking around.

"Hi," Allie said quietly. "You do look a lot better; you were really pale before, and you were burning up." She reached out to touch my forehead under my hair. She was here when I was sick? When was that? How come no one told me? I thought of Olivia—she had to know, she knew every time someone came to see me. And she didn't tell me.

"Let's all sit down. I brought sandwiches, and the nurses said we could have the TV room to ourselves for a bit." Mom turned my chair and led the group down the hall, toward the TV room. We went by my room, then Olivia's. I strained to look inside, but only caught the end of her bed, I couldn't tell if anyone was in it or not. Maybe she would come by the TV room to meet my parents. I was hoping she would, except that Allie was there, and that might be weird.

Mom rolled me into the TV room and over to the long table. Everyone else grabbed chairs and sat down. "Oh, I left the sandwiches in his room. I'll be right back," Mom said, turning to go.

Dad and Mike were talking about a football game that was on the TV screen. "I wonder if they'll let us turn up the volume," Mike said. "When I bring music in, those nurses practically have a stroke. . . ." Mike caught himself. "I mean, no offense, do they have, like, actual stroke victims in this hospital?"

Allie shot him a look. "Seriously, Mike."

"What? Who cares? It's not like any of them can HEAR ME!" He yelled out the last two words.

"You're not funny," Allie said under her breath.

"I've been here a few more times than you, so I think I know better what goes on at this place, okay?"

So maybe Mike did know that we'd broken up. I wanted to tell him that it was okay, that I was fine with it, but he wouldn't look at me. Instead he put his head down on the table for a moment.

"It's okay to be nervous, Mike, it's okay." Dad patted Mike on the back awkwardly.

Mike kept his head down, but I could still hear him. "It's this place, it just—it sucks, it's not right." Mike slammed his hand on the table hard, making the puzzle boxes rattle. "This whole thing sucks!"

Allie looked away, horrified. I knew Mike was embarrassing her.

"I'm going for a walk." Mike shoved his chair back and, without saying anything to me, stormed out of the room with his head down.

"We haven't forgotten how hard this has been on you guys," Dad said, moving over to sit by Allie. "It's hard for everybody, and I just really want to thank you for being here for West; it means the world to us."

Allie looked down at the table, sniffling. Jesus, was she going to start crying too? What kind of shitty surprise was this anyhow? She put her head back up just as Mom walked in with a deli bag. Whatever was in it smelled delicious.

"Where's Mike?" She looked to Dad, who shook his head slowly.

"He'll be back," Allie volunteered. "Here, let me help

you," she said, and took the bag and sorted through the sandwiches, handing them out. I watched her move around the table, carefully placing napkins and sodas by each person's place. I had been hanging out with Olivia for so long, I had forgotten how pink and bright Allie looked—her cheeks rosy from the cold, her curly blond hair glowing gold in the sunlight. She was gorgeous, there was no denying that, but Olivia had her own look too—a colder, darker kind of beautiful.

"So." Mom unwrapped her sandwich and looked over at me. "We told Mike and Allie about your surgery and they just wanted to come and wish you luck, right, Allie?" I noticed that when she talked to me, she spoke a little bit louder.

"Yup." Allie didn't meet my eyes; instead she focused on opening her soda, then glanced at me quickly. "I know it's going to go great, Mrs. Spencer, and . . . and then . . ." Allie paused and collected herself, I could tell she didn't want to cry in front of my parents. "Well, it'll be just like it was, everything will be . . . fine." She unwrapped her sandwich and put it in front of her, but I knew she wouldn't eat it.

Mike walked quickly back into the room and pulled out a chair, like nothing had happened. "Wow, thanks, Mrs. S, this looks awesome." He chomped into his sandwich and ate about half of it in two bites. "So who's in the room next to West? That kid's mom looks like a model or something."

"Please, don't talk with your mouth full," Allie said angrily. I could tell that she and Mike—who could barely stand each other when I was around to run interference—had not been getting along in my absence.

"I think it's a young lady; I don't know much about her," Mom offered. "Actually, I think she said she was a dancer—or maybe her daughter was a ballerina." Mom shook her head. "I can't remember."

"Is there a Mr. Ballerina in the picture?" Mike asked, his eyebrows going up and down a few times like a sleazebag.

"Seriously, Mike," Allie huffed. "Some respect? Her daughter is in the hospital."

Mike shrugged and bit into his sandwich, finishing it off. "I'm just curious about who's spending time with my man West here," Mike said, winking over at me. "That's all." He looked at Allie's skeptical face and grinned, wiping his hands on a napkin. "Thanks again for the sandwich; tasty," he said to my mom. "Next time I'm hanging with West, he'll be eating one, too, right, buddy? No more eating through a tube for you." Mike pushed back his chair and came over behind me. "Can I take him for a spin? Just down the hall, nothing crazy."

"Oh, I don't think so," Mom said quickly.

"Let him, it's just down the hall." Dad sighed.

Mom shot him a look but said, "Okay, five minutes, Michael."

Mike backed my wheelchair away from the table and rolled it slowly out the wide doorway. "Back in five," he said over his shoulder.

The second we were out the door, he started walking—and pushing—faster. "Damn, I hope that chick didn't leave already, you have *got* to see her." He stopped outside Olivia's door, peeking in. "Gonzo, let's see if she went this way. . . ." He raced down the hallway, pushing me way too fast toward the nurses' station. The second we rounded the corner, he slowed way down. "Hello, ladies," he called out to the nurses, who barely looked up. He rolled me over to the same double doors where he had come in.

"That's her," he whispered, leaning in close to my ear. Outside was a tall, thin woman in a dark coat, belted tightly around the waist. I noticed her legs first. Even though it was cold out, she had on fancy boots—black, with high heels. Then I saw her face. It was Olivia's face. It could have been Olivia—only older, with shorter hair and dark lipstick, eye makeup. The way she brought a cigarette to her lips and inhaled deeply, then blew the smoke out into the cold air, she looked like she was in a movie.

"Man alive, you didn't tell me about this chick, keeping the good stuff to yourself. Does her daughter look anything like her?"

I blinked yes before I could stop myself. A mistake. I didn't want Mike bugging Olivia, going into her room. I also didn't want Olivia to meet Mike, not yet, not until I'd had a chance to fill her in on what he was like. But then I realized something. Olivia wasn't like Allie. She could totally handle Mike. She would eat Mike for lunch. The thought made me laugh.

"Did you just say something?" Mike came around the front of chair and looked into my face. "That was weird, it was like you said something." Mike laughed but it sounded forced. "No, seriously." He studied my eyes for a second and I blinked no.

Olivia's mom had seen us watching her, and gave us one of those patronizing waves that you give to little kids. "Aw, busted. Way to go, wheelchair boy." Mike smiled and gave her a little wave back.

"Good luck tapping that later," Mike murmured, rolling me back to the TV room. "Actually." He leaned down and spoke close to my ear as he walked me down the hall. "Once you're out of this chair, I bet you can use this whole accident for a bunch of sympathy nookie. Or maybe that's just what I would do." We rounded the corner into the room and Mike put on a fake brightness. "Howdy, we are back from our adventure. I return with West, just as you saw him last, except now with a new tattoo."

I noticed that Mom and Dad were sitting closer together now, and Allie was right next to them. What had they all been talking about when I was gone? The room had an

136

awkward feeling, like we had interrupted something. Maybe Allie was telling them that she dumped me.

"We should probably let this guy get his rest, but thanks so much for coming, you two." Mom stood up and hugged Mike first, then Allie. Dad stood and cleared away the lunch stuff on the table. "I'll call you tonight," he said to Mom, pulling her in for a hug. It was still shocking for me to see my parents acting that way, like they still liked each other.

"Good to see you, West," Allie said, finally looking at my face. She seemed to be searching for something, maybe a sign that I still cared about her.

"Next time, two legs instead of four wheels." Mike kissed the top of my head hard and walked out the door beside Allie, without looking back.

"I'll be here for the big day next week, bud." Dad got down and looked into my face. "Stay healthy, okay?" He and Mom exchanged a wordless look as he walked out the door, and she sat back down.

"Your father flew in just for the day and then gave those two a ride up here." She finished her soda and put the empty can on the table. "To be honest with you, of all your friends, I think Mike is taking this the hardest. That boy." She shook her head slowly and looked out the window, staring at the same winter trees that I always looked at. "His mom told me he's been having a terrible time at school—fights, detention, you name it."

Detention wasn't anything new for Mike, but fighting was. Who did he get into a fight with? And why? I felt like he wasn't telling me anything real during our visits, just keeping everything light.

"Part of me thinks that maybe you help to keep him grounded; he really needs you as a friend." Mom looked over at me and met my eyes. "Just one more reason to get better."

As if I needed another reason.

Chapter 16

'm cold. I push my hands deep into my pockets, but my fingers are still numb. My toes are so cold, I can't feel them anymore, and it's getting dark. In the streetlight up ahead, I can see the snowflakes beginning to fall. I want to get home; I walk faster, with longer strides, watching my boots hit the sidewalk. But when I look up, it seems like I've gone the wrong way. Somehow, I'm downtown. I know this part of town, but it's far from where I live. In the distance, head-lights are coming down the street—a bus. The driver pulls to a stop, opens the door. "Getting on?" he asks. He's a big guy; his thighs spill over the driver's seat, and his meaty hand holds the wheel. That's when I see Olivia. She's sitting up front on the bus, looking down at me from the window. She's so pale, so sad. I'm happy to see her, but she's not happy to see me. She locks eyes with me and shakes her head no, silently, slowly. Her mouth doesn't move. The driver slams the door in my face and pulls away. For a second, I think that maybe that was Olivia's mom in the bus. But no, I can see hair, long and dark, down her back as they pull away. I know that was her.

"Got a smoke?" someone asks me, and I turn to see a guy next to me. He's older than I am, but I'm taller. He looks cold, in an old brown leather jacket, a ratty T-shirt, and dirty faded jeans. "Smoke?" he asks me again. I shake my head and he starts to walk away from me, but then stops, turns, and says, "I know you?" I realize, as the street-light hits his face, that I do know him, and he knows me. I've seen him before. "Man, I just wish I had a smoke." He pats the upper pocket of his jacket and that's when I see the blood. On his hands, the tattoos on his knuckles. The wrists of his jacket. Some of it is splattered on his face. "You sure you don't have a smoke?" He moves toward me again and then I hear something, a girl crying. It starts soft, but then it's harder, sobbing, gasping for air. There's someone on the ground, right by the bus stop, a girl lying on the ground, curled into a ball, crying. "You don't need to worry about that," the guy says, moving in front of her so I can't see her. "Don't worry about her; she's a waste of time."

———

"I didn't want to wake you," Olivia said, wiping her eyes, then blowing her nose. "I was just going to check on you. Sometimes, when you're asleep, I just come in here to make sure you're okay. I did that when you were sick. I just wanted to . . . to know you were okay." She grabbed another tissue and blew her nose loudly. I waited for her to make a joke, about stalking me in my sleep, about her unladylike nose honk, but it didn't come. Her face looked so serious, so sad.

It was dark, and the room felt cold, like they turned down the heat. "I know your parents were here today," she said, pulling her robe up around her knees and sniffling. "And I know Mike was here. And I know *she* was here."

She stopped for a second and looked down at the floor. "I'm sorry I'm such a mess. I just . . . my mom was here today and we didn't have a great visit. She saw you, by the way." Olivia smirked and caught my eye. "She said, 'What is that handsome boy doing in a place like this?'" She put on a faux French accent that sounded pretty convincing. Olivia took a deep breath and turned her head away from me, and for second, I was reminded of her mother, smoking outside. The same mannerisms, the same measured beauty. "Let's go for a walk?" She raised the back of my bed up until I was sitting, then dropped the leg rest. "I didn't know the part about letting you sit like this for a couple of minutes before you got in the chair," she explained. "I just learned that today."

I wondered how much of the rest of my parents' visit she had listened in on, how much she had heard, or seen.

"While you're getting adjusted, I've got something for you. I'll be right back." She went through the divider and left me sitting by myself in the dark room. I could feel that my toes were cold, my feet were cold. That was a new sensation, something I hadn't felt in a while, a little tingling.

She came back in a moment later, holding a manila file, like the kind they had at school. "Remember when we talked about this room, about your bad dreams—about how maybe the guy in here before had something to do with it?" She opened the folder and sorted through a few typed pages. "I have a picture of him. A couple of pictures. But I'm warning you, it's not pretty. Do you want to see?" I blinked yes and she glanced down at the photo before reaching over to my bedside lamp and clicking it on. She held up the picture so I could see it.

It was hard to tell how old the guy was in the photo. Maybe twenty, maybe older. Or younger. What was left of his hair was blond. He looked like a something from a horror movie: bulging eyes staring out of a skeleton face. It took me a second to realize he couldn't help the stare—his eyelids were gone. Part of his nose was missing, leaving a raw pink hole in the middle of his face. His lips were gone; just teeth were showing, the gums blackened. He had one ear, with a little patch of blond hair over it. On the other side of his head was just a ball of red flesh where an ear used to be. I knew at once this wasn't the guy from my dream. It wasn't the dark-haired guy with the blood on his hands. But I couldn't stop staring at the photo.

"Is it him?" Olivia asked. I pulled my eyes from the image and blinked no.

She turned the picture around and looked at it herself for a second, then tucked it back into the folder. "I'm glad it's not him, to be honest," she admitted. "I didn't want to think that he was haunting you, or this room." She got the wheelchair from the corner. "I guess I still feel bad, like I could have done more, should have done more for him. If it turned out that he was here as a ghost, that would be a sign that I was right. Does that make sense?" She moved in to hold me, to move me into the chair, her arm around my back, my chest over her shoulder. She lifted me and put me into the chair with more ease this time. "That orderly was right; your mom could do this for you. It's easier every time." She unhooked the IV bag and moved it over to the pole on the chair. "Now, let's see if I can get this right." She carefully switched off the respirator, reconnected the tube to the portable, and turned it on. I didn't skip a breath. "Okay?" She came around the chair and looked into my face for a second. I blinked yes, and waited for a smile, but I didn't get one. I was getting the feeling that Olivia was mad at me, or mad at her mom, or just mad. Maybe it was seeing that depressing photo of the burned guy. I wanted to cheer her up, like she had done for me so many times.

"I feel like I should have tried to be friends with this guy, this"—she paused and looked at the file lying on my bed—"Paul. Maybe I could have done something, noticed something, told the nurses."

I was thinking of the day I was running a fever and Olivia was the first one to notice it, to get a nurse. Maybe there *was* something she could have done for this guy, but who knows, maybe not. He looked like he was pretty bad off.

I blinked no at her. She couldn't beat herself up over this. "I'm having a shitty day," Olivia explained. "A lot of doubt, a lot of thinking." She clicked off the bedside lamp, moved behind the chair, and pushed me out the doorway, pausing to be sure we were alone first. The hallway felt warmer than my room; it felt good to be in the light. My room was creeping me out after seeing that picture of the guy who was there before me.

"I would say we should try for a midnight stroll, but it's about twenty degrees out there, so . . ." She pushed me slowly down the hall, then turned my chair into the TV room and closed the door behind us before pushing me over to the computer table and pulling up a chair.

The room was dark, but it wasn't as scary as my room, and I was happy for the change of scenery. "So I guess you heard me crying before, when you were asleep?" I wanted to blink yes, because I did have some idea, but instead I blinked no. I wanted her to tell me herself.

She curled up in the chair, pulling her robe over her legs. "I told you about that guy, Paul, how he had visitors at first. Then, slowly, they stopped coming." She paused and looked at my face in the darkness, studying my reaction. "When's the last time I had a visitor? Not my mom, I mean a friend. Anyone. Do you know?"

I tried to think, but I couldn't remember her ever having a friend come to visit. Her mom was the only person who came. I hoped that our little party today hadn't been what started her thinking this, but I was pretty sure it had. "You know why I don't have any friends visiting me? They stopped coming. They stopped coming because they want to see this girl." Olivia stood and struck a ballerina pose, up on one toe, her head cocked to the side. Suddenly, she twirled in a perfect circle on her toe, then stopped, looking me dead in the eye. "They want to see this girl." She danced effortlessly across the room, her robe flowing behind her like a white dress. She spun and danced back to me, stopping close to the chair. I could hear her breathing.

"They don't want this girl." She yanked up her sleeve, showing me her shunt, that angry piece of plastic shoved under her skin, held in place with medical tape. "They don't want to see the girl whose hair is falling out"—she grabbed her ponytail and came away with a handful of dark hair—"whose skin is pasty, the girl who doesn't smile." She leaned in, so close that I could feel her breath on my face, and gave me a hateful look. "Nobody wants this girl," she said slowly. She was so angry; I'd never seen her like this. And it frightened me.

She slumped back into her chair and put her head into her hands for a moment, then looked up at me. "So you know what was weird to me today? After dumping you, weeks ago, little blondie girlfriend just shows up here today, trots in like she owns the place, little powwow with the parents while your other buddy takes you on a stroll. The perfect girlfriend. Don't you think that's strange?" Olivia squinted her eyes and stared at me.

She turned to the computer and clicked it on. I was nervous about what she was going to show me. Did Allie have a new boyfriend? Was she going to show me something about my friends that I didn't want to see? She went again to the video site, and I watched as she typed in "BMX racing." When a list of videos popped up, she clicked the first one and sat back to watch it play. I didn't like watching it. Seeing other guys getting air and hitting jumps while I was in this chair was not my idea of a good time. Why was she showing me this?

"You know why Allie was here today?" She said Allie's name like it put knives in her mouth. "She was here because she wants *that* guy." Olivia poked her finger at the screen, pointing out the guy who was in the lead. He was in full gear, matching leathers and jacket, cool race helmet. "She wants that guy, and so does Mike, and so do your parents. And now, with this surgery, they think they're going to get that guy back." Olivia paused the image on the screen on a close-up of a guy hitting a corner hard, mud splashing from his tires and hitting the camera lens.

Olivia scooted her chair close to mine and her put her hands on the armrests. "They don't care how risky it is for you, that there's a good chance you'll die rather than be okay again. They don't care, because that's how much they don't want this." She poked my chest hard with her finger.

"Allie dumped you because she wants the biker guy, she wants the handsome guy, she wants to *walk* down the hall with that guy, Mr. Popular"—she pointed at the screen again—"not this guy"—she hit my chest hard and I flinched. "Did you feel that?" she asked, surprised. "You did feel that, didn't you? See!" She jumped up from the chair and spun around again, suddenly happy. "The doctors said you would get feeling back on your own, if you just waited, if you were patient. You don't need this surgery next week. You don't need it! You can get better slowly, safely—we can get better together. Me and you. Here." She smiled for the first time all night and knelt down in front of me, lifting my hand to her face, placing my palm on her cheek. I wished that I could feel it, feel her softness, her warmth, but I felt nothing.

"I don't care how long it takes, because I love you, West. I love *you*." She emphasized the last word, making it clear that she didn't care what state my body was in. Moments like these, when I was dying to wrap her in my arms, being trapped in this body was so frustrating, it was torture. What she didn't understand, what I was aching to tell her, was that I wanted to get better not just to get back to my old life, but for her, too. I wanted to help her get better, to get out of here. Wasn't that what she wanted? For both of us to be free of this place?

I looked into her eyes. She had just told me that she loved me. That wasn't lost in everything else. I heard it. And I loved her, too. As crazy and complicated as she was, as insane as it was to fall in love with a girl you've never actually talked to, we were in love. It was that simple. And she was worried about me. But she didn't need to be. I knew it was all going to work out. I just had to convince her.

"And the dreams—your dreams, my dreams—about this place, about that guy. Those aren't an accident. That means something. I know you want to just brush it away and forget, but you know it's all connected. We're connected." She put my hand back down and laid her head into my lap, sighing.

Then suddenly she pulled her head up to stare at me.

"I have an idea. Let me talk to your mom. She'll be here tomorrow. Let me just talk to her for two minutes. I think there's stuff in your file that they aren't telling her. Stuff that I looked up online. Things she might not know."

Did I want Olivia talking to my mom? She had been on the fence about the surgery from the beginning. A concerned patient telling her that she had looked into my file, seen something there . . . it wouldn't take much for my mom to change her mind, to pull the plug on the whole thing. A few words from Olivia, and my chance for surgery, for getting out of here, would be over.

I blinked no.

"No, you don't want me to talk to your mom? Does that mean you'll tell her that you don't want the surgery yourself?"

I waited a moment, terrified of Olivia's reaction.

I blinked no.

"What do you mean, no? You're just going to do it— you're just going to let them cut you open?"

The way she put it sounded so barbaric, but I had to blink yes. I wanted the surgery, no matter what.

"So even after all this, after everything I'm telling you, after everything I've done for you. You know, I could have gotten in a lot of trouble looking in those files; I could get in a lot of trouble for just being in your room, much less taking you out like this." She motioned to the room. "After all that, you're telling me you want to go ahead with it? You're ready to die for these people, for what they want you to be?"

Olivia was wrong. I wasn't going to die, and I wasn't doing it for them. I was doing it for me, for us. I couldn't stay here forever with her like this. I wanted out, whichever way out was.

She watched my face and then shook her head. She stood and walked to the windows, putting her hand on the glass. "And what about me? I'll still be here, and someone new will be moved into your room, someone who's been in an accident, someone who needs a friend. And I'll have nothing left to give, because you will have broken my heart." She sniffled and I could hear her crying again, quietly. "I guess I mean nothing to you. How I feel means nothing to you; you're just going to do what you want—what they want. And I go back to being stuck here, alone."

I blinked no, but she wasn't looking at my face. A memory washed through my mind. A girl crying, cleaning out a drawer in my room. Was that Olivia? Was she crying and taking out my things after . . . after I was gone? No, that was just a dream, the ghost of a dream, a nightmare. That girl was a child, smaller than Olivia, younger. It didn't mean anything.

I was going to come through the surgery, I was going to be okay, and I was coming back here for her. Whatever happened, I was coming back here for Olivia. She might not believe that now, but it was true.

"I thought you were different. But you're just like them." She stood behind my chair and turned me toward the door. "I should have known better," she said quietly, as if to herself.

Who was she talking about? Her friends, the ones who never visited her? I wasn't like them. Just because I was choosing to take a chance on myself, on the surgery, that didn't make me selfish. I had to do it. But she was right about one thing. I had taken her for granted. The visits, reading to me, sneaking files, the whiteboard, her patience, listening to my dreams, taking me on midnight walks. I pictured her pushing my hair from my eyes—how many countless times had she done that? Curling up with me in bed, even if it meant the nurses might catch us. Telling me I could do it—that I could write, I could feel, I was still West. I was important, I was still alive. Olivia had done that for me. She had been my connection to the world of the living. Someone who I felt real with. The only person I felt real with.

Olivia pushed me back to my room in silence, quietly and slowly put me back into bed, moving as if she were in a trance, an emotionless robot. After putting the wheelchair away, she lowered the bed back down so I could lie flat, and arranged my hands carefully. Then she leaned over me, pushing my hair back from my eyes, her hand trailing down my face lightly, along my cheek, a butterfly touch.

"Good-bye, West," she whispered, as if I were already dead. I blinked no, but she didn't see it, or didn't care anymore.

Chapter 17

When I woke up the next morning, it was a bright winter day—the kind of day where the sun seems too white, too stark, and you imagine for a second that you're on another planet, in a sci-fi movie. The clock read only 9:30. Was it Sunday or Monday? I couldn't remember at first. Then I did. It was Sunday. Yesterday was Saturday. Mom and Dad and Allie and Mike. And Olivia. Her face last night, that kiss, her telling me good-bye. But she didn't mean it. I knew her, just like she knew me. And I knew that any minute I would hear the divider slide open, and she would be there, pulling her IV stand behind her, looking down at her feet, feeling shy because of how she had acted, the things she had said last night. She had told me she loved me. Not that it was a surprise—it was one of those unspoken things between us—but still she had said it, and that meant something. I knew exactly how much it took to say that to someone, to be the first one to say it, because of Allie.

One afternoon, after school, we were walking to the bus stop—I didn't really need to stay after school that day since my work on the sets was pretty much done, but I did anyhow. I used some excuse to stay and watch Allie onstage. She was good, I had noticed before, but now that we were hanging out, I felt this overwhelming sense of pride watching her move onstage, deliver her lines. She slipped into character so smoothly, from joking around backstage to really being the girl she was supposed to be in the play. I imagined her famous someday; it could happen, she was talented and really pretty. And there was just something about her, she had that special thing that made you want to get close to her. I'm sure I wasn't the only person who noticed it.

When we left the school two hours later, it was freezing out, almost dark, and we walked close. Allie was wearing that puffy blue coat. She looked like a blue marshmallow with a white hat on; cute, even though I knew she didn't think so. I kept grabbing her, squeezing her, hard enough to push the air out of the down jacket, but it would just puff right up again. "Knock it off." She laughed. "Put me down!" but I kept doing it until she was almost actually annoyed with me.

While we waited at the bus stop, I stood behind her and put my arms around her waist. She leaned back against me and we were quiet. Even though it was freezing out, I felt totally happy, just standing there with Allie, listening to the sound of the snow settling into the cold. When I look back on it now, I get it: we were alone. There weren't any distractions, so she was mine, for that moment. I was thinking about Allie onstage, and the Allie I had in my arms. My heart swelled with pride just being with her. I felt overwhelmingly lucky—blessed. I saw the bus coming in our direction, slowly making its way up the slush-covered hill, and I leaned down and whispered in her ear, "I love you." She spun around, quickly, a shocked look on her face. "I'm going to kiss you now, okay?" She smiled—this was an old joke, from the night that we met. We had talked and talked for what felt like hours at the party, and then, in the middle of a conversation—I think she might have even been mid-sentence—I couldn't take it anymore. I just blurted out, "I'm going to kiss you now, okay?" She stopped talking and just sat there, shocked, as I leaned in and kissed her on the lips, our first kiss. Later she told me it was one of the sweetest things a guy had ever done with her. I didn't want to think about the other guys, and how many she had kissed, but I took the compliment.

I heard the whine of the bus brakes beside us, the door swing open, and we climbed on, holding hands. I didn't realize until I had gotten home, until I was sitting at my desk doing homework and daydreaming about Allie, that she hadn't said anything back. She didn't say anything back for a long time.

It took a while for me to realize that Allie was always a little reluctant to be my girlfriend. It seemed like she wanted to be chased, or maybe she wanted me to be unsure where I stood with her. Mike sometimes joked that Allie kept me on a leash, like her pet. When she snapped her fingers, I came running. When her ring tone sounded on my phone, Mike would sometimes make the sound of a whip snapping, as I scrambled in my pocket to answer before she hung up. Allie wasn't the type to leave you a message if you missed her call.

I guess that was part of the thrill, part of the excitement when she finally did give me anything—any sign that she genuinely liked me. But a lot of the time, especially lately, just before my accident, I felt like things weren't solid between us. Like if I screwed up at all, if I didn't call her back fast enough, if I spent too much time biking with Mike, if I did anything wrong, that she was going to dump me again and go back to that poem-writing asshole or to some other guy. It always seemed like there was someone else waiting in the wings. I didn't know who they were—or even if there really was a guy, but it just felt like it. That's how she made me feel, like I could be replaced. Like I always had to earn my shot at being with her.

"How we doing today?" The bitchy nurse pulled me from my thoughts as she leaned over me and checked my pulse. I couldn't believe it, she actually said something. She never spoke to me, well, almost never. She must have been in a good mood. She touched the tube on my IV, adjusting something, then wrote some numbers on my chart. When she was done, she left without so much as a smile. But at least she said something.

The nurse was the first person in my room today. I knew she would go into Olivia's room next. If she was still asleep, the checks would wake her up. So I could expect her any minute. I heard some talking in the next room, but it was too soft for me to make out who was speaking, what was said. When the talking stopped, I stared at the wall and waited for the sound of the divider. Instead, I just watched as the shadows grew longer and the sun moved across my window. Then it was afternoon, and still Olivia didn't come, didn't open the door, didn't do anything in her room—I would have been able to hear her.

The sound of a cart in the hallway on rattling wheels, the noise of my respirator pushing air in and out, in and out. I listened to everything, waiting to hear—anything from her. Moving in her bed, talking to a nurse. But she was quiet. I could picture her, in her bed, exactly how she must look, her cheek on the pillow, one hand tucked underneath, looking out the window, her long dark hair spread out behind her. Her face would be pale, the color drained, the way she looked sometimes when she had been pulling out her IV a lot. Her lips a light pink, making her eyes seem even darker.

I knew she was thinking about me right now, while I was thinking about her. If I closed my eyes, I could see her face so well, imagine it, how she looked right before she smiled, how her eyes would light up first. Her hands, small and white. I could feel her thoughts, and I knew they were of me. Olivia was right, we were connected on some other level. We didn't need to always talk. We could just know. It wasn't like what I had felt for Allie, that constant chase, the missed connections. Something about being with Olivia felt complete. A quiet calm. It was love, real love; I finally understood what people meant when they said they were in love with someone. I got it now. This was it. I had found it, with Olivia. Or maybe she had found me. Whatever had happened to bring us together, I was thankful for it. I knew how crazy that sounded, because it wasn't like I was thankful for my accident, for going through all this, but in some way I was thankful. How else would I have met this girl, and been in this place long enough to know her? It was meant to be.

As the light in my room turned from golden to dusk to dark, I didn't feel anxious. I let go of that feeling. I waited, but I knew she would come. And if she didn't come today, she would come tomorrow. I knew it because I knew her and I loved her, like she loved me. It wasn't just a word, like it was with Allie. It wasn't just a sometimes feeling.

I heard Norris's voice in the hallway, at the nurses' station, and I knew that night had come; a whole day had passed without Olivia. I closed my eyes and pictured her, standing by my bed, touching my cheek. It was only a matter of time.

Chapter 18

I can hear her breathing. She's here with me, beside me, asleep. All dark and white, her pale skin with hair tangled around her shoulders, spread over the pillow. She's wrapped in the sheet. The room is so cold, I want to pull up a blanket for her; it's at the bottom of the bed, but I can't reach it. My arm won't move; it's numb. I try to hold my hand up to my face but I can't—it's tied down. I'm tied down on both sides. "Olivia," I whisper. "Olivia." Something changes in the corner of the room—something moves. Out of darkness, I can see an outline of someone, a man. I can see the light at the end of his cigarette as he takes a drag, and I smell the smoke. His face in profile is not normal—it's distorted, blackened with burned skin. His nose is gone, his eyes bulge from lidless holes in his face, staring at us. His lips are pulled back, burned away in a menacing grin.

The bed feels hot now. It's too warm; it's burning, black smoke pours from under us. It's not his cigarette I smell; it's us. We are on fire. The room is on fire, the bed. Still Olivia doesn't move, she's curled up but so deeply asleep. He just stands there, watching us, as flames crawl across the floor, darting out from under the bed like snakes. "Olivia!" I try to roll, to shake her, but she's motionless. I can hear the fire now, it's under the bed, licking at the sheets, sucking air. Over the sounds of the flames, I hear laughing.

———

"You can't smoke in here! You know that." The voice came from the next room, Olivia's room.

"Oh, *pardon moi*, I'm so sorry, really," I heard Olivia's mom say in her accent.

"With all the oxygen tanks we have in here, do you understand how dangerous that is? An accident waiting to happen." It was the voice of the bitchy nurse.

"I was just in Europe, and things are so different there. Forgive me. . . ."

"I don't think they smoke in hospitals, even in France," the nurse said curtly as she wheeled her cart into the hallway.

I listened for her mom to say something else, but once the nurse was gone, all I could hear was the soft sound of someone crying. Was something wrong with Olivia? What if that's why she didn't come to see me yesterday?

After a few moments, I heard the sound of a chair being

moved, a window closing, then talking. I couldn't make out what was said, but no doubt Olivia was pissed at her mom for being gone for a while. She was probably asleep when her mom showed up, or pretending to be. Her mom just lit a cigarette, out of habit, while she was waiting for her to wake up. That's probably what happened. I could picture her mom standing at the windows, looking out over the frozen grounds, a cigarette artfully poised in her hand.

As I was straining to catch any sound from next door, Kim walked into the doorway. "Hey, stranger," she said brightly. "Our last day together." As she took my chart from the bottom of the bed, she rethought what she'd just said. "I mean, not in a bad way! Just that you're in surgery Wednesday, and if all goes well, and I know it will"—she winked at me—"then you will be going on to physical therapy somewhere else, probably at . . ." She paused and looked at my cart. "At McArthur Med. Oh, that's a great center." She looked at me sadly for a minute, and I couldn't tell if she was genuinely going to miss me or if she held the same belief that Olivia did—that I was going to die during the surgery, and this would be the last time she would see me.

"Well," she finally said awkwardly, "don't think I'm going easy on you today, mister, it's going to be the full routine. I don't want you getting to McArthur next week and embarrassing us both." She pulled the sheet up from the bottom of the bed, exposing my legs and feet. "Looking pretty good, much better; you're almost all healed here." She ran her hand over my leg, where the giant scrapes had been. I could feel it, her touch on my leg. It didn't feel totally normal, but I could feel it, the light pressure; things were coming back after all. She bent my right leg at the knee, then extended it. As she bent it again, I told my muscles to make the same motion.

"Excellent!" she exclaimed. She looked almost startled as she met my eyes. "You're making progress; this is really something!" She bent my leg again, then straightened it, with me pushing along. "You can feel that, right? You're doing that, aren't you?" she whispered, leaning closer to me. She looked into my eyes. "West, can you straighten your leg on your own?" She bent the knee again and left it that way. "Go on, push it straight," she ordered. I tried, but my foot felt almost jammed against the sheets, like I couldn't get it to slide. "Come on," she whispered, and I finally did make it move a little bit, a few inches, but not totally straight.

"Okay, that's something!" she said. "I'm going to go and get the doctor; you stay put." When she realized what she'd said, she started to laugh. "I mean . . . you know what I mean." She left the room and I tried again to hear what was going on next door. But I heard nothing, meaning that Olivia's mom had probably left. And now she could hear everything going on in my room.

A young doctor walked into the room, with Kim close

behind him. He didn't say hello to me or anything, just moved to the bed and looked down at my legs.

"It's not going to look like much, but remember this patient has had no motion below the chest, so . . ."

"I have a ten thirty," the doctor said curtly.

"Of course, okay." Kim seemed totally flustered as she bent my left leg. "West," she spoke loudly, "I just want you to try and straighten this leg now, like you did on the other side. Just as much as you can."

At first, I did try to move my leg. But then I stopped myself. If I did it, and the doctor saw it, would that mean they would cancel the surgery? That I would be left to regain movement on my own—at this snail's pace? And what would Olivia think? I knew she was listening to everything from next door, waiting to see what they said.

I decided not to try. I couldn't do it anyway. I needed the surgery. I wanted the surgery.

"Well," Kim said quickly, "maybe he can only do his right leg. Let me show you." She straightened my left leg onto the sheet and moved around the bed.

"I have to go; I'll come back and examine him later when I have more time," the doctor said as Kim set up my right leg.

"Just watch, give it a second, he just needs a minute," Kim said. "Now, West, do what you did before. Straighten this leg, push it straight for me. Straight down, you can do it." The look on her face broke my heart, but I did nothing. After a couple of seconds, the doctor looked at his watch. "But he did it before, he did," Kim said sadly.

"Like I said, I'll stop by later today, thank you, Ms. Lassig. Keep up the excellent work." The doctor turned and left the room, leaving me and Kim there looking at each other.

"You know what? That's okay," she said after a moment. "I saw it. I know you're not strong enough to do it again, but I saw it, and I think you're doing great." She gave me a weak smile as she bent and straightened my leg repeatedly, stretching the muscles in and out. I let my leg go slack and allowed her hands to do all the work. I just hoped Olivia hadn't heard too much.

After she worked both my legs, she moved on to my arms, and I closed my eyes, I didn't want to be a part of what was going on with my body. I didn't want to check in and see what I could feel, what I couldn't. I didn't want Olivia to be right. But I was beginning to think she might be. When Kim was done she quietly took my chart and wrote on it for a few minutes, then she moved beside the bed. She must have thought I was asleep because she leaned in and took my hand. "I'll be thinking of you on Wednesday. I hope it all goes great. I know it will," she whispered, and then she was gone.

It was time for checks, but after that, I knew that Olivia

would be in to see me. She had heard what Kim said to the doctor, and I was sure she wanted to gloat; she wouldn't pass up that opportunity. But after the carts went up and down the hall and were parked back at the nurses' station, still the divider stayed closed. She didn't come.

The afternoon bled into evening, and the next person in my room was Mom. I must have dozed off because she woke me asking, "Does it smell like cigarettes in here, or is that my imagination?" She sniffed the air, then leaned in close to my face, smelling around my head. As if I could be smoking. "Well, as long as it wasn't you," she said, and grinned at me. "I guess I have bigger things to worry about than my teenage son smoking, don't I?" She sighed and pulled the chair closer to the bed. "So the plan is that I'll see you tomorrow night, then Wednesday morning, I'll be here for the transport. Not sure yet if I'm going with you in the ambulance or if your dad and I will just follow behind. The ambulance isn't going to be racing along, sirens blaring, by the way, it will just be driving normally, so you don't have to worry about your mom being able to keep up!"

I could picture her in the old Volvo wagon, pedal all the way down, leaning into the steering wheel. It was funny, but the sad part was I knew she would do it for me. I imagine she drove like that the day when I had the accident. When she was on her way to the hospital, probably wondering if I was even alive. I felt like shit for all I'd put her though. I just wanted to get out of here, get everything right again, make it up to her. As if she could read my thoughts, she leaned in and whispered, "So this is it, huh? This is it, we're really doing this."

As she spoke, I had this sudden awful vision of Olivia in her room, standing right behind the divider, listening, waiting for the chance to open the door and step in, my medical charts in her hand, ready to talk to Mom, ready to talk her out of it at the last second.

Mom kept talking, but I couldn't get the image out of my mind. "I don't have a lot of time tonight. I'm taking Wednesday and the rest of the week off, so I have to finish up this proposal tonight and get it in tomorrow." Mom looked out the window, like she was mostly talking to herself. "I just wanted to come by and say hello to my sweet boy." She smiled at me and put her hand on my forehead for a moment.

"They'll take your blood tomorrow, just to make sure everything is okay, but I know it will be. You don't have to worry about that." She took my hand and sat there, holding it for what felt like the longest time. "Oh my, I'm just lost in thought here, I'd better go home," she said finally, tucking my hand back under the covers and pulling the blanket up to my shoulders. "I'll see you tomorrow," she said, kissing me on the head. "First thing after surgery, we are getting you a haircut!" she joked, pushing my hair back again. As she left the room, I listened carefully, waiting to hear Olivia move from her room, to follow Mom down the hall. I had this terrible feeling she was going to do it, try to catch my mom at some moment and confront her, convince her. But instead I heard Mom's voice at the nurses' station, talking to Norris on her way out, a laugh, then quiet.

Once I knew she had gone, I was able to relax. Maybe Olivia wouldn't do that; maybe she was coming around to my side of thinking. Maybe she had listened to me after all, had listened to what I wanted.

Still, I waited for her after Mom was gone, I waited for her to come in and confront me about what she had heard earlier. About what Kim had seen, and what that might mean. But when Norris came in with my night meds, she still hadn't come. She had to come tonight, she had to. Tomorrow would be my last day here. She had to come. There just wasn't any other way.

Chapter 19

My last day at the hospital passed just like all the others, except without Olivia. The blond-haired nurse gave me a sponge bath in the morning, put a fresh robe on me, and made my hair incredibly dorky by combing it straight back and parting it on the side. The young doctor who had been in with Kim the day before was true to his word and came in to look me over. He spent about five seconds looking at my chart, then bent my leg quickly under the sheet, extending it out a few times before just putting it down. He flashed a penlight into my eyes. "Looking good," he said as he jotted something on the chart, then left. I was sort of dying to see what he'd written. What did "looking good" mean? But the only person I could ask would be Olivia.

I hadn't seen Olivia in three days, though it felt like

longer. It was like I could feel her anger through the wall; she was still stewing about it. I had figured a day or two and she'd be back. But she wasn't. She could hold a grudge—I knew this already, from how she treated her mom. Sometimes her mom would come to visit, and if Olivia was mad at her she just wouldn't speak to her. I don't know if she pretended to be asleep or if she just lay there defiantly in her bed, but I know she didn't talk when she was here. She would also sometimes give nurses and even doctors the silent treatment. When I first got here, one of the nurses had mentioned Olivia's terrible behavior, her temperament, saying something like "she's a piece of work." Or were they talking about her mom? I couldn't remember now, but it suited her perfectly. A piece of work.

I was trying hard not to let it get to me, but I missed her and I felt like I needed to see her before I left for surgery. Seeing her and feeling her support would probably help me get through things, but I tried to tell myself I didn't need it, that I would do okay either way. Because I knew it was going to work. And then I was coming back here, on my own two feet, and she was going to be blown away. Besides, everything she thought—that the surgery wasn't going to work, that I was going to leave her or forget about her—everything she was worried about was going to be pointless, and then she wouldn't be mad anymore. How could she be?

Instead of focusing on the fact that she was still pissed

at me, I used my secret biking technique of thinking positive thoughts. I had learned about positive imagery in my tenth-grade psychology class. The teacher, Ms. Lunn, was a total loony tune, but there was something about this unit on the power of the human brain that really stuck with me. Ms. Lunn told us this saying: If you think you can't, then you can't. Which just means that if you convince yourself that you can't do something, then of course you're not going to be able to do it. I read the chapter called "Think Into Being" in our textbook twice; it was about using the power of your mind to make things happen in the real world. There was a visualization technique in the book that I started doing, too. Whenever I was trying to get a new bike routine down before a competition, I would practice it over and over again in my head.

I would sit quietly somewhere, close my eyes, and picture every step of the routine—every move, where to pedal fast, where to slow down, how to lean my body—and I would watch it like a movie in my mind. I was always careful to picture the finish, too—that last moment when I would cross the line. It was important to picture that, to soak in that good feeling that you get when you've executed something perfectly. I would go so far as to picture the judges' scores sometimes; what numbers I would see, what numbers I wanted to see.

I never told Mike about this technique, but I did start

to see some changes on the track. The more I focused on what I wanted to have happen, the more it happened. It wasn't magic—more like confidence building. You can only spend so much time on the track, but the more you do a routine, the better you feel about it. So picturing it every day, even on days when I couldn't get on my bike, gave me more practice time, in a way. When there was a really tough move I thought I couldn't get, I would focus on just that trick, over and over in my head, until I could do it in real life. I noticed at the last competition, I just felt more confident while I was riding: *I've done this before, and it goes great.* It was like I had tricked my brain.

For the past couple of days, I had been trying to picture Olivia coming into my room, sliding open the divider door, her bashful way of looking down at her feet, how she would smile at me. But no matter how much I pictured it, it didn't happen. Then I realized something. You can't use your mind to make anyone else do anything; you can only work on you. So I decided to change my thinking and focus on the surgery. I tried to run through the whole thing, every step of what would happen, what was going to happen from the moment I opened my eyes. I would be able to reach up and touch my own face. I would be able to move my legs. I didn't know what type of physical therapy I would be in for afterward, so I couldn't really picture that. Instead I just saw myself walking. I saw myself with Olivia, visiting her here, holding her. I saw myself coming into the hospital, through the sliding doors by the nurses' station, and how happy Nurse Norris would be to see me standing, walking, healthy—the way I used to be, the way I would be again.

The movie playing in my head was interrupted only a few times—a nurse came in and tied off one arm. I knew what came next, and now that I could feel it a bit, I did dread it. But maybe this would be the last time. "Just a little prick," she murmured as she drew a few vials of blood. The mean nurse came in later and checked my chart, my pulse. She didn't speak to me. Then in the evening, Mom showed up as planned, just around the time the night nurses came on. "I've got something special for you," she said, digging into her bag.

She had four or five greeting cards, the first one from my uncle John and aunt Kate and the twins. It had a picture of a bear on the front, in a hospital bed in all sorts of traction and looking miserable. "I can *bearly bear* the thought of you in the hospital. Get better *beary* soon!" Mom read. "Cute, huh? I bet Benjamin and Felix picked that out." She moved on to the next card, from Dad. He would be here tomorrow. There was a card from Mike with a hot nurse on the front.

"Well," Mom said, blushing, "I guess he means well." One from Allie. She had made the card herself and painted a watercolor on the front. "This is the one I just couldn't believe; it came yesterday." Mom held it up for me to see. A huge card with a pretty regular "get well soon" type thing on the front, but inside was covered with signatures—must have been a hundred of them—all over the back, too.

"It's from the junior class at Marshall, can you believe that?" Mom said. "Some people wrote little notes: 'miss you' and 'get well soon, cutie'—who wrote that?" Mom peered closer at the card to see the small signature.

Mom put the cards up next to the bed so I could look at them overnight. "I'll be sure to get these in the morning, when we head out. Speaking of . . ." She glanced at the clock. "I have to go, we've got an early day tomorrow. Your surgery is at eight, so . . ." She leaned in and gave me a kiss. "I'll see you in the morning. And just you remember"—she motioned to the cards—"you've got all these people counting on you, thinking about you. We all love you." She grabbed her coat and bag and turned to go before I saw tears.

"Oh, Mrs. Spencer, I am so happy I got to see you tonight!" I heard Norris say just outside my room. They talked for a few minutes in the hallway, I couldn't make out everything they were saying, but eventually I heard Mom call out, "Thanks again for everything, absolutely everything," as she left.

A few moments later, Norris came into my room with my nighttime dosage. "So, handsome, there's a rumor going around that you want to leave me, huh?" She smiled and gave me a wink. After she injected the contents of the syringe into the IV line, she sat next to me. I felt the drugs flow into my arm, cold and fast. I was already feeling fuzzy when she sat beside me on the bed and took one of my hands. "I am going to miss you, Mr. West, and that is no lie. But I am happy for you. Get out of here and get back out there," she said softly, looking out the window into the darkness. "This is no place for the living."

The last thing she said sounded in slow motion and her words rang in my head as I drifted off. I wanted to be running through my movie, my positive thinking as I fell asleep, but I couldn't focus. I could only feel her hand, and hear her saying the word *living* like she was saying it over and over again.

Chapter 20

I'm at the lake, sitting up on the bluffs on a blanket. There's a girl with me, but it's not Olivia. It's not Allie either. It's a girl I've seen in a movie, but I can't remember her name. She's pretty; she's wearing an old-fashioned bathing suit and it looks good on her. I feel like we're in a movie together, like we're being watched. There are cameras. "Tell me again what happened," she says, and runs her fingers down my back, touching scars. I notice a man standing near us; he's dressed like he works at a doctor's office, in scrubs. Before I can ask him what he's doing here, he says, "Let's go." That's when I see another man standing on the other side of our blanket, and together they lift the whole blanket, with us on it. We tumble together, she's laughing. "This isn't right," I tell her. "Let us out!" She keeps laughing; it's all a big joke to her. I'm screaming, but they carry us and keep carrying us, to the edge, to the bluffs. I know they are going to drop us over the side. But I'm ready. When they drop the blanket, it falls open and I feel myself weightless, tumbling. The girl is gone, but I get ready. I put my arms out to dive— if I can hit the water right, I won't break anything. I'll be okay. But I'm falling and falling forever; it's too far. I open my eyes, knowing that I'll see the water far below me, and the rocks.

———

"It's bumpy back here, isn't it?" Mom said. It was dark, we were moving, jerking forward. "We'll be there soon; it's only twenty minutes, they said." She looked worried, her face tired and lined. From the back windows I could tell we were in the ambulance, driving. The sunrise was red and pink, bright like a grapefruit. *Red sky by morning, sailor take warning.* But I'm not going on a boat, I'm going into surgery. What does that red sky mean?

All at once I remembered the dream, and the feeling of being lifted. I was still pretty drugged up when the orderlies came to get me this morning, but I remembered it now: the two guys sliding me into the back of the ambulance, Mom getting in. Dad was there, too. He must be driving behind us; that's why Mom kept checking out the back window every time we took a turn. "Almost there," Mom whispered.

And Olivia. Was that a dream, too? No, it was real. I saw her. She came to me, like I knew she would. Last night. I woke up and she was beside me, watching me sleep, curled against me, her long hair tangled around her pale face. She said my name over and over again and touched my face until I was awake enough to see her. But it wasn't a dream. The memory washed over me as I dozed off in the ambulance.

"I know it's your decision to make, your life. I know that now, but I have one thing I have to ask you," she whispered. "Come back for me. No matter what happens, come back for me." I blinked yes quickly and watched her face. "No matter what," she said sternly. Her eyes were almost terrifying in my dark room; I couldn't see any emotion on her face. I blinked again and she curled up beside me, holding my hand. "You won't leave me here. Don't leave me here, West. Promise me." I could hear in her voice that she was crying. "Please come back for me, come back for me."

Most people I knew, even adults, would never admit that they were scared. Or that they missed you. Or that they really loved you. Why were people so afraid to say things like that? Why was I? It wasn't cool. It showed weakness. But that didn't make sense. It actually showed that you were strong, that you were real. I loved Olivia for teaching me that. And there was no way I was about to forget her, or not come back to her after the surgery, no matter what happened.

"I know you will, I know you," she murmured as we fell asleep together. I didn't even worry that Mom or the nurses would come in early the next morning and find her there, sleeping against me, because it didn't matter anymore—what could they do to us?

The ambulance backed into a loading area at the hospital as Mom said, "We're here!" brightly. She rubbed her hands over her face and glanced at her watch. "Seven thirty, plenty of time."

When the orderlies parked, they came around and opened the doors, letting Mom get out first, then pulling me out feetfirst. They put the wheels down and rolled me through two big double doors. The guys went to talk to the hospital officials while Mom stood beside my bed. The portable ventilator must have been somewhere, under the bed or attached, because I could feel it pushing air into my lungs in a steady rhythm. Dad walked in just as the guys were ready to wheel me into the elevator. "You'll have a chance to say good-bye upstairs," the red-haired guy said. "But they're ready to take him right in."

"Okay," Mom said. I saw her holding Dad's hand in the elevator as we made our way up. When the doors opened, they rolled me out and down a long hallway where we ran into Dr. Louis.

"Hello, good morning, welcome, how are we doing?" he said.

"We're nervous but ready," Dad volunteered. I heard Mom gasp out a sob. Dad hugged her in quickly and she cried hard into his shoulder. "She's just . . ."

"It's hard, I know," Dr. Louis said. "But remember, things are about to get much easier. This is what we have to do to move forward from this place, and you don't like being here; you don't like West being like this." He looked over at me on the bed like I was a rotten steak he wanted to send back. "It's time for us to help West, all of us. Isn't it?"

Mom stopped crying long enough to nod her head as she wiped her nose.

"And so we will," Dr. Louis said with a quick smile. "The nurses will show you to the waiting room, which is down the hall. You can wait there. They will also give you a beeper so we can contact you if you are on another floor; they will explain everything. In a few hours, we'll know more." Then the doctor turned to the person standing behind him. "Can you take him to OR, thank you."

"Wait!" Mom said. "I have to say something first." She leaned over me and looked into my face. "We're right here, can't wait to see you after. We're right here, West, the whole time, okay?" I blinked yes and saw the relief wash over her face. I could tell, she was suddenly strong. Maybe the doctor's pep talk had worked.

"Go get 'em, West," Dad said awkwardly as they rolled me away. Once we were in the large white operating room, things moved quickly. There were five or six people there, and they all moved efficiently; sometimes I couldn't tell whose hands were on me and where. One person was swabbing my arm for a needle, another was checking my trach, someone was injecting a syringe into my IV. They all talked to each other as if I weren't there, as if I were asleep already, or invisible.

"Have you seen this procedure before?" one woman asked.

"Amazing." The guy standing over me nodded. "Dr. Louis is the real deal, brilliant. I just wish he'd take on more residents."

The woman shrugged. "Some of them don't like a bunch of students asking questions, you know, they just want to do their thing."

"All right," the man on my left said as he capped off my IV tube, "this guy is not waking up anytime soon." I knew what he was talking about a moment later as I felt whatever he had injected into me take hold—icy cold in my veins, my mind fuzzy.

"Can you check the tray for a small punch forcep?" someone said, and I thought for a second they were talking to me. I turned my head to look for it, whatever it was, but that side of the room was suddenly empty. On the other side, everyone was gone too. I was alone. Where were they? I could hear music playing softly, classical music, and it felt so good and warm to just lie there. When I closed my eyes, I saw a hazy blue light, as if I were at the beach. I noticed Frankie, my old golden Lab, was down by my feet, keeping my legs warm, keeping me company. I hadn't seen him since I was eight, when we'd had him put to sleep. "Frankie," I said. "Good dog, that's a boy."

Chapter 21

I'm coming down the escalator at the mall. I'm so high up I can see everything. I can look around and see everyone, what everyone is doing. They are all like characters in a video game, moving around busily, like ants. Standing still and watching everyone else move makes me so happy; I love the feeling of calm washing over me. No one even sees me there. I'm coming down the escalator for a long time and I want it to last longer and longer. I close my eyes.

———

The sun on the lake is so bright that even with my eyes closed I can feel it coming through my lids, sparkling off the water, the reflection like mini-fireworks twinkling. Her hand is on my back. "Tell me again," she says, "what happened." She runs her hand over the scars. When I turn, I can't see her face. I shield my eyes from the glare, but I see only a shadow of a girl sitting next to me—her silhouette, a black cutout.

———

Someone is crying. "No, no." A girl is crying, sobbing. "Don't, don't . . ."

Olivia.

———

A phone is ringing. "How do you turn this off?" someone is saying. "They shouldn't even have this in here."

Mom.

———

I couldn't see, couldn't open my eyes. I heard shuffling noises—someone was near. My hand came up to my eye, and I felt . . . tape. A thick piece of tape from eyelid to mid-cheek. I tried to pick it off, but then I stopped. *I'm dead. I'm dead, and when I open my eyes, I'll be in a coffin, in a morgue.*

"Oh, you want that off?" a voice said. The tape was peeled back carefully and I saw a face, a woman I didn't know. "Hi, I'm Tracy. I'm your nurse." She spoke very slowly and carefully. "You're in the hospital; you've just had surgery." She peeled the tape off the other eye and I could see the entire room. "You were in an accident. Don't try to talk; you have a trach tube in. You're breathing on your own so we're going to remove that tomorrow, okay? Raise your hand if you can hear me." She smiled when my hand went up.

"Stay calm, I'm going to get your parents; just relax." I raised my hand again.

My hand.

I looked at it. It was my hand.

I moved my toes. I bent my knees up. Something jabbed in my stomach, hard. I felt around and found a big tube, like a vacuum cleaner tube, taped to my side and going into my lower abs. It hurt like hell to touch it.

My head was pulsing with pain. It felt like there was a band around my forehead, like a hat that was on too tight. But when I reached up to take it off, nothing was there.

"West!" Mom raced into the room, "Oh, honey, how are you? How are you?" She looked terrible, like she hadn't slept in days. "How do you feel, oh, you're moving! Look at that"—she turned to Dad—"he's moving! He's moving!"

A huge grin spread over Dad's face. "Well, they said it went great, but it does feel good to actually see it with your own eyes, doesn't it?" he said. Mom was jumping up and down like a cheerleader, yelling with excitement. She stopped and tried to collect herself. "How do you feel, do you feel okay?" she asked.

I moved my hand up to my head and touched my forehead.

"Your head hurts?" she asked.

I pointed to my forehead again, then made a thumbs-down sign. "Okay, I understand," Mom said quickly, but weirdly she had this huge grin on her face, like me being able to tell her I had a headache was the best thing that had ever happened to her. She put her hands over her face and started crying again.

The nurse stepped around them and held up my wrist. "I'm just going to check everything out, West," she said, then turning to my parents, said, "The headache is very common with this type of procedure; it's more like a migraine from a spinal tap. I have something I think will work, but I think the doctor is going to want to see him before we administer that." Then she turned to me and asked loudly, "Did you understand that, West?" I raised my hand, but my head was hurting so bad I had to close my eyes.

"We'll give him the dose right away, because it does take a while to work and we don't want him in this much pain. It will make him a little groggy for a few hours," she explained.

"But he can't fall back into a coma, can he?" Mom asked.

When she said that, my eyes flew open. Had I been in a coma? How long ago was the surgery?

"No, he's okay," the nurse reassured her. "He's doing absolutely great, in fact; this medication will just break the headache, nothing else. Let me go get that. You all can visit for a few minutes until Dr. Louis gets here."

Mom pulled a chair over to the bed and Dad stood

beside her. "Can you feel your toes?" she asked, so I pulled my legs up to show her. The tube in my stomach really killed, too, so I pointed to it.

"That's a feeding tube, to make sure you were getting enough calories," Dad said quickly. "Did they say that would come out with the trach tomorrow?" He turned to Mom.

"Oh, I don't remember." Mom looked flustered. "Dr. Louis said something about being able to swallow—let's ask him when he gets here. West, you're so skinny already, we want to make sure you can eat before they take the tube out." When she spoke to me, the volume went up. Why was everyone talking to me so loud?

My head hurt so bad that I felt like I could see sounds. With my eyes closed, I saw sparks when a loud cart wheeled down the hall. In a minute, the nurse was back with something in a syringe. "This should do the trick," she said, injecting it into my IV.

Mom was talking away nervously. "You don't know how nice it is to be able to have him tell us how he feels—I mean, it's been three months! I'm just so happy, I can't even tell you. When did Dr. Louis say he would be here?"

"He's on his way; let me go see if he responded to the page we sent him," the nurse said as she left the room.

I got the feeling she was psyched to get away from Mom, who was acting like a crazy lady. Why did Mom keep saying three months—it hadn't been that long. Maybe a month. Was it longer? I was confused; my brain felt scrambled.

Mom and Dad sat down while they waited, and spoke in murmurs. I could see that they were sitting next to each other, heads close together. I could catch only snippets of their conversation; I didn't want to hear it. My head hurt too badly, and the medication wasn't helping yet. Finally, slowly, I started to feel the band around my forehead loosen up a little bit. But I also started to feel like I was drifting off. I remembered Dr. Louis coming into the room and talking to Mom, then asking me to lift my hands, to touch my nose, but it all felt like it was happening in a dream. I did my best, and he seemed happy with that. "You just rest now, West. He needs lots of rest, then we'll be able to gauge where we go from here." I drifted back to sleep hearing Mom talking to him, Dad asking some questions. I felt good, warm and sleepy, and I knew that everything was going to be okay.

When I woke up, the room was darkened, and I was alone. My first thought, now that my head felt better, was of Olivia. She was going to be so happy to hear that I was doing fine, that everything had worked. I had to have Mom or Mike call her right away. I drifted back to sleep thinking of what she might say, and how soon I could see her.

The next morning, Mom was there again when I woke

up. "Hi, sweetie," she said when I opened my eyes. "They are going to take you in for a brief surgery just to remove the trach and the feeding tube. The doctor said it's a fifteen-minute procedure, at most, but you're ready for it today, okay?"

I gave her a thumbs-up. Then I motioned that I wanted to write something by pretending to hold a pen and writing in the air.

"Oh, you want to write? Okay . . ." Mom searched her purse and found a pen, then took a card off the bedside table and held it up for me to write on the back. My hand was pretty wobbly, but not as bad as it had been before. I wrote *Olivia*.

"Who's that?"

Then I wrote, *Tell her I'm OK.*

"Is this someone Mike would know? Or Allie?"

I wrote *Mike. He knows. Hospital.* I knew Mike would remember the pretty girl from the room next door. *Have Mike tell her. I'm OK.*

By now I was exhausted and my giant scrawl had filled the back of the card. Mom took it and tucked it into her purse. "I'll call him when you're in surgery and make sure he gets the message," she said. "How's your head? Is it better today?"

I gave her an okay sign with my fingers just as two order-lies came into the room to wheel me into surgery. "This is a quick one," one of them said. "We'll have him back in no time." Mom grabbed my hand before they took me out.

"I'll be right here, sweetie." Exactly what she had said last time.

The guys wheeled me down the hall and into an operating room much like the one I was in last time, only with less people. A guy in a mask leaned over my face. "Hi, West," he said loudly. "Today we're going to remove your trach. It's a fast procedure, but it can be painful, so we're going to put you under for this. When you wake up, don't try to talk right away. Let's give it a day or two, okay?"

I gave him a thumbs-up to show him that I understood. He nodded to a woman who was standing by my IV stand. I didn't even have a second to feel myself falling asleep, instead I just woke up back in my hospital room. I thought for a moment that they had forgotten to do the surgery, that something had gone wrong, because not enough time had passed. It felt like one minute. But when I reached up to my throat, the brace was gone, the tube was gone— now it was just my neck, skin, and a big bandage taped down over my lower throat. The feeding tube was also gone, a small bandage in its place.

Mom wasn't in the room when I woke up, so I decided to try talking. "Hi," I said to the empty room. It sounded very froggy, not like my voice at all. "Hi," I tried again, but air came whistling out under the bandage on my throat, making it almost impossible to say anything. Before I could try it again, Mom showed up and Dad was with her.

"That was fast, and you're already awake." Mom was staring at the bandage on my throat. She moved down the blanket to peek at the bandage on my stomach. "He said three stitches." She turned to Dad. "Out next week."

"Looking good, buddy," Dad said, taking a seat next to me. "How do you feel?"

I raised my hand to make a sign, but then decided to give it a go, to try to talk. "Okay," I said. My voice was low and raspy; I sounded like a creepy whispering guy from a horror movie.

Dad's grin said it all. Mom turned away so I wouldn't see her crying, but I knew she was crying again. "The doctor was just telling us that if you place your fingers here"—Dad took my hand and put two fingers over the bandage on my throat—"the air won't come out quite as much and you can talk a little bit more."

I tried it, pressing down just a little. "Hi." Definitely better, louder.

"Like that." Dad smiled. I knew it was hard for him to look at me, his son, covered in bandages, thin, and with long, greasy hair that stuck to my forehead. His face looked pained.

"But he also said give it a day or two to close up; they don't put stitches there," Mom added.

"Olivia," I said, pressing down on the gauze again.

"Oh, yes, I had Mike tell her that you were okay," Mom answered. "And she was very happy to hear it." She gave me a little smile. "I'm sure he'll tell you more when he's here this afternoon. I think he was a little surprised to hear that you knew her at all. And you know how we all feel about Allie. . . ."

"I should go get the doctor, right?" Dad said nervously. I could tell he did not want to get into a conversation about my girl problems right now—or ever. Mom nodded and he left the room.

After he walked out, Mom took my hand and scooted closer to me. "I'm so happy, I can't tell you how happy I am. I wasn't sure this was going to work, that we would get you back after all this time," she started.

The doctor walked in with Dad behind him, a huge smile on his face. "This is exactly what I want to see, my friend," he exclaimed as he adjusted the bed up. "You're going to find that talking is difficult for a little bit, until this closes up." He peeled back the bandage on my throat. "Looks wonderful. This can take a week or a little more, okay? Your vocal cords are like every other muscle in your body, and we're going to give them all time to come back; you've been immobile for long enough that you'll need physical therapy to get back on track. Do you understand?"

Without the brace and trach, I found that I could nod my head easily now.

"Wonderful. So my colleagues and your parents will talk to you more about the schedule and where you'll be going next. We find that patients who start therapy immediately come much closer to a full recovery, and that's what we want for you."

I nodded again.

"Okay, so"—he turned to Mom and Dad—"we are ready to move him on Thursday. Until then, it's rest and we'll just monitor his progress."

"Thank you so much, Doctor," Mom said, grabbing his hand in both of hers and shaking it up and down. "Thank you."

"Shall we?" He motioned to the hallway and they followed him out. I closed my eyes, but I could catch a little of what they were saying. Watching for infection, the medications I was on. Then the doctor said something about "overwhelming" me. At first I thought he was talking about doing too much physically, but it was clear from the conversation that they were talking about overwhelming me in other ways—mentally. "Unless he asks you directly . . . ," I heard him say. Then something about ". . . will come back to him slowly, when he's ready." Were they talking about the accident, because I remembered that clearly, the bikes at the quarry. Mike's face over mine, looking down at me, asking me questions. Mike's eyes, so close up, his pupils like tiny dots in an ocean of bright green. "You're okay," he kept saying. "You're going to be okay." I fell into a druggy-haze nap thinking about the accident. Had something else happened that I couldn't remember? Something they were worried about? I ran over everything in my head, watching it like a movie. The way I fell. Mike. Allie crying and crying. I could see all of it clearly. But what I couldn't remember was whatever happened next. How did I even get to the hospital? Did Mike take me in his car? Did they call an ambulance? I tried to think, but there was nothing there. Just blackness. Not even a dream memory. Until I woke up at Wilson and met Olivia. Everything that came before was lost.

Chapter 22

Mike's eyes, his pupils big this time, were directly over my face when I woke up. He backed away quickly when I jerked awake, like I was Frankenstein's monster come to life.

"Holy crap, they weren't kidding. You really aren't a vegetable anymore. Can you talk?"

I put my fingers over the gauze. "How's this?" I rasped.

Mike grinned. "Well, that's sort of like talking," he joked. "It is good to have you back!" He pulled over the chair and sat next to me. "I can't get over it. You really are okay, right, you can move and everything?"

I lifted one leg, then the other, like a good student, then held up my middle finger. That's what he gets for calling me a vegetable.

"Nice." He smiled. "You seem to be back to yourself." Mike sat and stared at me for a few moments, nodding, like he was wondering what to say. I didn't know what to say either.

"So, I don't know how to ask you this except to ask it: is your brain okay?" he finally said.

I gave him the finger again as an answer.

"Okay." Mike smiled shyly. It was weird, like we were getting to know one another again. When Mike came to visit me at Wilson Center, he seemed more himself. What had changed? Why was he being so serious now?

"Here's why I'm asking." Mike looked down for a moment. "Because your mom told me you wanted me to tell Ollie Hudson you were okay. And so, I did it, but man, really? Since when? Forgive me, bro, but that chick is nasty. She's got a mustache. I heard she has the herp, down there." He pointed to his crotch.

I realized he thought I had meant Olivia from our school.

I put my fingers over the bandage. "Not her." I shook my head and motioned to the pad and pen Mom had left beside the bed. I had been told not to talk too much, but it was pretty hard to get across what I wanted to say in just a word or two. I quickly wrote, *Olivia Kemple, from the other hospital. Long dark hair, room next door.*

Mike took the pad from me and looked at it for a

second, then looked up at me. "The girl next door to you, at Wilson?"

I nodded and took the pad back to write more. I had assumed he would know I was talking about her—I don't know why. Stupid mistake.

"So your parents told you I visited you there," he said as I kept writing.

I put my fingers over the bandage. "I know." I had to keep clearing my throat to talk, it wasn't easy. I handed him back the pad, where I'd written more information about Olivia, and what I wanted him to tell her.

"West—" Mike started to say something, then looked at me. His face was superserious. "See, this is what I'm talking about. You couldn't know this girl from that hospital. It's impossible. You must mean somebody else."

He handed me back the pad and gave me a sad look, like I was crazy now, or brain damaged.

I covered my throat. "Can you call her? Now?"

Mike shook his head. "Look, there's no girl. You must have, like, I dunno, dreamed her up or something. Everyone on that floor was a vegetable, including you."

No, I wrote, with a ton of exclamation marks after it. I didn't understand why he was being such a dick about this. *Olivia, next door, room 203. Call her.*

Mike took the pad, read it, then closed his eyes and put his head down a second. "West, the whole place was people connected to machines. I know, I was there. It was pretty funny, cause I would bring in some tunes for you, and one time this nurse—"

I interrupted him. "Norris."

"Anyway, she was like, 'Can you turn that down,' and I was like, 'Did someone complain'—get it? Because there was no way any of those vegetables had a problem with me playing . . . wait, how did you know the nurse's name? Big lady?"

"Norris," I said again. "I remember." I took the pad and wrote, *You played Water Gun album, you talked about a new girl you liked, Erin, who wore a skirt.* I passed him the pad.

"No . . . no, there's no way."

Mom rounded the corner just as Mike looked like he was going to lose it. "Hi, boys! So nice to see you two together, like old times." She smiled. Mike stood up, his face white.

"Something really weird is going on. West remembers stuff. He remembers me coming there, and the music and even Erin's skirt—this is freaking me out." He spoke so quickly my Mom could barely follow what he was saying.

"He remembers what?"

"Everything! He remembers when I visited him, when he was in the coma, he knows the nurse who walked in! What she looked like—her name!"

As Mike was talking I wrote more stuff down on the

pad, but I stopped when I heard the word *coma*. Why did he say that? Had I been in a coma, maybe after the surgery? It didn't make sense. *I know every visit, when you all came and put me in the wheelchair, when you took me down the hall—I wasn't a vegetable.* I shoved the pad at Mom and pointed to the last sentence. "Tell him," I said.

Mike read it over Mom's shoulder and they both looked at me. "Do you remember me coming to visit you?" Mom asked.

I nodded and covered the gauze. *"Harry Potter,"* I rasped out. *"A Separate Peace."*

"Oh my God." Mom had tears in her eyes. "Wait, I've got to go and get Dr. Louis if he's still here. This is amazing. I can't believe this!"

Mike sat back down and shook his head. "I'm telling you, you were . . . *gone.* They had you hooked up to a bunch of machines. I wasn't sure you were ever coming back."

I took the pad from his hands and wrote, *No, I was awake. I was blinking for yes and no—you saw me! I want to call Olivia now.*

Mike looked at what I wrote and took a deep breath. "I don't know. . . ."

I pointed to the phone and said, "Call Wilson now."

Mom and the doctor came back before Mike could pick up the phone. "So I hear you've got quite the recall from your time at the Wilson Center," the doctor said. He leaned over me and checked my pupils with a pen light. "No headache?"

I shook my head.

"So you can remember your parents and friends visiting you while you were there?" I nodded, and he went on. "And specific things that were said to you?" I nodded again. He turned to Mom. "This is not unusual, actually, and it goes back to what I was saying earlier. He'll start to have these memories, almost like a dream coming back to you in the morning. He may remember great detail about one incident or one day, then have several days or weeks that are completely absent. It's the case with a level four or five coma; we don't know much about when they are cognizant and when they aren't, but it sounds like your boy had a lot of brain activity, which again doesn't surprise me given his age and general good health." He smiled at me, then patted my shoulder. "You'll be surprised at what you can remember, but mostly you'll surprise your family and friends, who thought they were talking to themselves." He laughed. Mom and Mike both laughed, too, but I didn't get what was so funny. Clearly they thought I had been in a coma or something—that I had been asleep, but I wasn't. I remembered everything.

"How about when Allie and I got in that fight? When she was complaining about my driving, and then I just left her there, and she had to wait for a ride—do you remember that?" Mike asked.

Allie and Mike fighting, in my room, together? I searched my mind, I didn't . . .

"And that nurse came in, the bitchy one, and was like, 'Visiting hours are over,' and Allie was like, 'This is all your fault,' because we were late." Mike paused and looked at my face, like he was looking for recognition. "And then she was trying to make it seem like I caused your accident, too, like I had dared you or something, and I didn't talk to her for a month after that, just so you know."

I didn't remember it at all.

I didn't know what he was talking about.

"How about Uncle John and the boys, do you remember that?" Mom asked quickly. "They flew in just to see you; they would be so happy to know that you actually heard them and knew they were there." Her face was so open and hopeful, I wanted to say yes, but I couldn't.

I didn't remember them coming.

I didn't remember even hearing about it.

Why didn't I remember?

"Well, three months is a long time," the doctor added. "Some of this will come back to him in time, and some won't. The brain is an interesting organ; the way it heals is, in large part, still a mystery to us."

Mike and Mom were nodding, enthralled with what the doctor was saying, while I could only focus on one thing: I had been in a coma. The whole time at the other hospital. They were saying three months. But I remembered things

201

too clearly. Or did I? Some days blurred together, sure. There were drugs and those terrible dreams and the hazy mornings when I felt like I couldn't wake up. But then there was Olivia, and she always helped me to get it together, to feel alive.

"Olivia," I said, pulling Mike and Mom from their conversation with the doctor. "I want to call Olivia." I pointed to the phone.

"Okay, sweetie," Mom said calmly, reaching for her cell. I saw Mike shaking his head. "You don't have her number?" she asked him.

"He says it's a different Olivia. She's at the hospital. She was next door to West." Mike shrugged, then looked to the doctor.

"I thought Olivia went to your school?"

I shook my head. "Call," I asked her. "Call Wilson. Olivia Kemple."

Mom looked over at the doctor as she got out her cell and dialed the hospital. The room was quiet for a moment until Mom started talking. "Oh hi, this is Cathy Spencer. My son was a patient there. . . . Oh hello, yes, he's doing wonderfully, thank you. He wanted to talk to another patient there"—Mom paused to look at me—"an Olivia Kemple." Mom listened intently for a few seconds, then said, "And you're sure this is Olivia Kemple?"

"Room 203," I said.

"He says she's in 203?" Mom added, then said, "Okay, well, thank you so much."

She clicked her phone shut and looked over to the doctor again. "Well, there is a patient there named Olivia Kemple, and you're right, she's in room 203, but how you know that, I have no idea." Mom shook her head.

"If she was in the room next door, he could easily have heard her name mentioned and remember that, or have a memory of voices in her room, people talking to her. There's a variety of ways he could be aware of another patient," the doctor started to explain.

I covered my gauze. "I want to talk to her."

"I would really prefer if you used the pad for now, talking in a day or two," the doctor reminded.

"It's okay," Mom cut in, "he can't talk to her. West, she's a coma patient. They couldn't put her on the phone."

"No," I moaned. "No." I felt sick. What had she done? She must have pulled out her feeding tube, done something to herself. What did she do? Then I suddenly realized, she didn't think I was going to make it. She did something— tried to kill herself. I didn't realize she was being so serious. I didn't realize.

"West." Mom took my hand. "She's in a coma, like you were. She's been a patient there for two years."

"No," I said. "I know her." I was going to throw up. Something felt wrong. Something wasn't right about the information they were all giving me. Someone was playing a joke. I hadn't been in a coma. I just couldn't move. Olivia wasn't in a coma, I saw her: walking around, talking to me, to everybody. Nurse Norris would remember, she would back me up. I tried to think of a time when Norris had seen us together, or talked to Olivia. There was that night in the hallway, when she caught her, the night I had my first bad dream. But was that Olivia? I couldn't see who she was talking to. I searched my mind: I couldn't remember a time when Olivia was in my room and anyone else saw her; she always raced out when the nurses came, didn't want to get caught, to get in trouble. And when people came to visit her . . . she never spoke. But that was only because she was angry. She was angry at her mom, at the doctors. But she did talk, sometimes, didn't she? I couldn't remember. Things weren't adding up. But I knew her. I knew her voice, her face, her touch, the smell of her hair.

"She's not in a coma," I said, and the doctor leaned over and handed me the pad and pen.

"Writing for now, okay?" he said, like I was a little kid. "We want to let that incision heal up nicely."

I flung the paper across the room, sending the pen flying against the wall. "No, I want to talk to Olivia!" I rasped out. "Call again."

"Oh, honey," Mom started to say, then she turned to the doctor. "What can we do?"

"It's normal to be frustrated, West," he said to me. "In

time, these memories that you have will weave together, and you'll be able to make sense of them, but as you're getting them now, in bits and pieces, I'm sure it's confusing and—"

I clamped my hand over the bandage and yelled: "Call her now." It felt like something in my throat tore open. I tried to sit up, jerking the IV tube so hard I almost pulled the bag down. I barely felt it rip out of the back of my hand. I couldn't just lie here and listen to these people talk about stuff they didn't understand. I wanted to talk to Olivia.

"Okay, let's calm down," the doctor said, pushing back on my shoulders, forcing me to lie back in the bed. I saw the slick warm blood where I had torn out my IV. "West, I need you to calm down, it's okay." Suddenly a nurse appeared in the doorway. "I need ten cc's of fentanyl stat," the doctor said. He used a different voice with her and she disappeared quick.

Mom looked terrified. Mike stood beside her, his face ashen. "Take a deep breath," the doctor said.

"I just want you to call her," I cried. "Just call her." I started crying and couldn't stop. Everything was ruined. Everything I'd been living for. The whole reason I wanted this surgery was to be with Olivia—to get to my old life back, but with her in it. And now she had done something terrible. I just needed to see her. "Just call her," I said again, as the nurse returned with two male aides. They held me down while the doctor injected a needle into my thigh.

"This will help you to calm down, West. When you wake

up, you're going to feel a lot better." He turned to Mom. "This type of agitation is normal; it's the central nervous system trying to get back on track after months of inactivity. It can take a while for things to settle down. You can let him go," he told the two guys who were holding me. When they released me, I had no desire to fight; I couldn't even form words. My tongue felt like putty, my head fell back, and I rolled into darkness.

Chapter 23

The next two weeks were awful, maybe the worst of my life. I had wanted so much to be better; I had wanted to regain feeling and movement so much that I had wished for it, focused on it, thought it into being. When I was in the hospital, it was all I could think about. Getting better, getting out, getting back to my old life. I even blocked out all the warnings from Olivia, from my mom. I pushed ahead for this, stubbornly, blindly, without considering anything or anyone else. But now that I was here, all I wanted to do was go back. Back to a place where Olivia was my only friend, where seeing her face could make my day, where hearing her voice was the only thing keeping me sane. A place where I could feel her touch, she could curl up beside me, be with me. Because now, that was impossible. And if

I believe what everyone tells me, it never even happened. But I know it happened.

A few days after Mike's visit, I was moved into a rehabilitation center where specialists worked on my movement—walking, using my arms, talking, and fine motor skills. There were other patients there; they were all older than me. Some had been in accidents—one guy had been in a terrible car accident a year ago and was just now learning how to walk again. A lady Mom's age who was there had a pretty bad stroke, half of her body didn't seem to work right. It was interesting to hear everyone else's story, what had brought them to this place, and I got the feeling most people considered me the star—I was the youngest and I had come out of a long coma. The other patients seemed really interested in that. About half of the patients lived at the center, and the other half just came in for appointments. "Pretty soon, that will be you," one of the therapists told me. "You'll go to outpatient pretty quickly if you work hard."

My days were full, from flash cards in the morning with a cognitive specialist to a walk on the treadmill, and then weights, protein drinks and meals packed with calories, Epsom salt baths and deep-tissue massage. Mom joked that I had the life of a pro-athlete now—my body was the priority. Getting it to work normally again was the goal. The doctors were working on my mind, too, but it was clear that what was wrong with me there would be much harder to fix. My memory had problems—big holes of time, lost to being in a coma (or so they told me) and damage to my central nervous system. I had visions of disturbing things sometimes, when I was falling asleep: a bloody girl lying on a sidewalk, a burned man's face—things that I had no control over, visions that had nothing to do with my life or my accident. The psychologist they brought in told Mom I was "depressed."

It seemed like my body would return to normal. "You're young," the physical therapists all pointed out. "This will all come back to you, muscle memory." Due to the synthetic bond they had used to fuse my vertebrae, I would never be able to touch my toes or tie my shoes standing up. My body would not bend that way completely, not ever again. I would be able to walk, hopefully someday without the jerky movements I made now, and I would be able to hold a pen. I would never be able to ride competitively again. I knew this and yet I didn't care. My garage full of bikes and gear—the equipment I had saved months for, the trophies and titles— all seemed like they belonged to someone else. A kid, a dumb kid. I didn't want any of it anymore. I told my mom to give it all Mike, if he wanted. Or to donate it. Nothing held any interest for me, least of all riding.

"I just don't understand why he isn't happier, when we're all happy for him," Mom complained to the doctor. "It's like he doesn't understand how lucky he is."

"He's a teenager. This is a difficult thing to live through, even for an adult. His life was already in transition, and now this on top of it. He will come through it, you'll see."

For the first few days, I still talked about and asked about Olivia. Was it possible that she had been okay when I was there and then fallen into a coma later, after I left? The answer was no. Could she have also been in the lightest state of coma, stage five, like me, and that maybe we were more aware than people thought we were? Again, no. The more I asked about her, the more insane I seemed. Mom finally called the hospital and got the answers I thought I wanted. She found out that Olivia Kemple had been in a stage one coma for two years. There was no way I could have known her, could have talked to her. It was impossible. Yet I knew it had happened. And I had to find a way to get in touch with her, wherever she was. It was as simple as that.

When they brought in a psychologist, I knew I was in trouble. They even interrupted my walking time on the treadmill for a meeting with her. In our first meeting, she asked a lot of pointed questions about my time in the hospital, and what I remembered. When we got around to Olivia, I tried to hold back. I knew that everyone thought I had imagined our entire relationship. That it didn't happen, that it was a dream. And until I could prove them wrong, talking about Olivia just made me sound crazy. Maybe I was. But then I gave up. Because if I couldn't tell a psychologist, who else could I talk to about it? Maybe she knew something I didn't. Maybe she had some explanation for how this could have happened. How I fell in love with a girl I'd never met.

"There was a girl in the room next door to you," the doctor started. "What was her name?"

"Olivia." The moment I said her name, I finally couldn't hold it back, so I spilled the whole story. Everything. How we met, how mean Olivia was at first, how she helped me communicate and write. The midnight walks, the TV room, the things she showed me on the computer. How angry Olivia was when I left. The doctor listened intently without questioning or interrupting. She never said, "That couldn't happen."

When I was done, I looked down at my feet, and the stupid Velcro braces they put on my legs to help me walk. "I don't want to be here, I want to be back there, with her, if that makes sense."

"It does make sense, West. It makes perfect sense. This is hard work, a lot is expected of you. This is the real world. You've been through something awful and traumatic, and you're very lucky to be alive. Now comes the work of putting your life back to together. It won't be like it was before, will it?"

I felt tears come into my eyes. She was right. I got what I wanted—what I thought I wanted—but now I didn't want it, or it hadn't come true the way I thought it was going to. I had wanted everything to go back the way it was. But there wasn't any getting back there now. That life was gone. This was my life now.

"I'll tell you what I think might have happened, and then we can work through how to get on the same page, okay? I think when you were in the hospital, you found yourself in such an unbelievable situation, such awful circumstances that you created another reality, a fantasy life that you could escape into. You needed a friend, someone who could understand what that was like. And then Olivia appeared." She stopped talking for a minute and just looked at me, to be sure her words were soaking in. They were. "Being with Olivia helped you, didn't it? She helped you." The doctor looked down at the pad on her lap. "You said she was your only true friend, the only one who understood what it was like for you. Is that right?"

I nodded. What she said did sound right—but it also sounded crazy. Because that would mean I invented Olivia. That she wasn't real. That everything that happened between us was fantasy, pretend. And *that* I couldn't believe.

"Tell me, West, did you have any dreams while you were in the hospital—dreams that were separate from your time spent with Olivia? When you would consider yourself asleep—things that you would say *weren't* real?"

I had to think for a minute, then it came back to me,

suddenly. The dream of the man attacking a girl. I told the doctor about the series of dreams about the girl, about the man hurting her. About me turning into him. "I had this dream over and over again—it was the same man, always. I can still see his face."

She nodded. "It wouldn't surprise me to learn that the man you dreamed about was a real person—maybe an orderly at the hospital, a male nurse or even a doctor. Someone whose face you saw and pulled into your thoughts." She paused for me to think about it, but I couldn't remember ever seeing this guy at the hospital. "Think about the dream. A woman is being attacked. What does that mean?"

I thought about it. "She's being hurt, she's being forced. . . ." I didn't know what answer the doctor was looking for.

"Yes, she's being hurt and forced. She can't stop her attacker. She's powerless. A lot of the procedures that were done on you while you were in a coma were invasive—they hurt, but you were powerless to stop them, weren't you?"

I remembered the dream more clearly. "Actually, I was always there watching, but I was tied down, I couldn't help her. My hands were . . . I was powerless. Even when she was screaming for help, crying . . ."

"I'd like you to think about the procedures that were done on you—including this most recent one. How much you felt like you were not in control of your own body, how much other people controlled you, did things to you when you couldn't stop them, and how that felt. Sometimes you were aware of it—a nurse giving you a shot, manipulating your body. . . ."

As she spoke the images came back to me. Someone leaning over me, checking my pupils, rolling my bed, shifting me, changing my IV. Constantly being touched, monitored, probed, tubes going in and out of me.

"Think about that in terms of your dream, and think about who this 'man' might be, and we'll pick up there tomorrow, okay?"

After she left, my head was spinning. I went back on the treadmill and walked an extra mile, just thinking about everything she had said. Was there an explanation? Was it as easy as that—a fantasy world of my own invention? A girl who did exist, a patient at the hospital, but whom I'd never met. A girl who was in a stage one coma. I had just heard her name, from the room next door, and I pretended she was beautiful, pretended that she was my friend. Invented a girl to go with the name. My imaginary friend. My imaginary girlfriend.

But every time I started to think that maybe it could have happened that way, I would see Olivia's face, her white robe cinched tight around her small waist, those big dark eyes. That time when she put on lip gloss, when her hair was down. I could see her so clearly, feel her breath on my face, her kiss on my lips, I knew she was real. I couldn't have invented her. I didn't make her up.

The next time the psychologist came, I tried to be open to her theories, especially about the dreams. There had to be some explanation. "We thought the room might be haunted, but I think your idea makes more sense," I told her.

"Who's we—you mean you and Olivia?" the doctor asked.

I nodded.

"So you talked to Olivia about the dreams, and she helped you with those, too?" When I said yes, I saw her write something down on the pad of paper she kept on her lap. Without looking up, she went on. "I want you to know that you can continue to talk about Olivia with me and you don't have to be uncomfortable. You understand that, right?"

"Yeah," I said. "I'll be honest with you, I want to believe that you're right about her. Part of me thinks you could be, but the other part of me just can't believe it. I just can't let her go," I explained.

"Let's take a look at what you said—'I just can't let her go'—that's important. If it's true that Olivia was a friend that you invented to help you through a rough time, why do you think it would be hard for you to 'let her go'— especially now that you're doing so much better?"

I thought about it for moment before answering. "Because I fell in love with her? I made her promises?"

The doctor couldn't hide her disappointment in my answer. "Maybe because you're worried the hard times aren't over. And it's going to be difficult to return to your old life, isn't it? You've told me before that you almost wished you were back there, at the hospital, rather than facing the life that's in front of you, isn't that right?" When I nodded she went on. "Maybe it's easier to keep that friend for a little bit longer, just in case. When you're ready to let go of Olivia, you'll know."

I didn't think I'd ever be ready to let go of Olivia, of the idea of Olivia, even if she was right. But I hoped for something to happen soon, some kind of realization—one way or the other—before everyone around me started to believe I was insane. Including me.

Chapter 24

After two weeks of exercises every day, I finally felt I was getting somewhere, like I was moving forward. I had pretty good upper-body strength; I could lift things over ten pounds and hold a pen for fifteen minutes. Typing was still hard, especially the little buttons on my phone—getting them just right took a long time, so when I sent a text to Mike or Allie, it was usually full of misspellings. Probably made me seem like my brain damage was worse than it actually was.

My mind was coming back too, but the doctors said that would be slower. It took a while for the tissue there to regenerate, and I had done some damage when I crashed. Mostly it was short-term memory issues—I would leave the room and walk down the hall, then forget where I was going and why.

"Well, now we're alike," Mom joked. "That happens to me at least once a day. I'll even pick up the phone, then forget who I was going to call." Hearing this made me feel a little bit better. Sure, it happened to everyone. But it didn't used to happen to me, and I didn't like the confused feeling I got when I was unsure of what was going on. I tried to use my mental imagery to focus myself, to help my concentration. But that was like a joke—I would lie in bed and try to picture myself being back home, or back at school, to propel myself into a brighter, better future where this was all behind me. But thoughts of Olivia and the other hospital would weave their way in.

Whenever I thought of Olivia or something reminded me of her—which was about twenty times a day—I tried to block it out. "When those thoughts come into your mind, try to gently replace them with something positive," the psychologist had told me. "Something else. Like what sort of activities did you used to enjoy?"

"Mostly biking," I told her honestly. "But I won't be doing that anymore."

"Anything else, any hobbies . . ." When she saw me shaking my head, she went on. "How about swimming?"

When she mentioned swimming, my mind went to the bluffs, overlooking the lake. Allie and I used to go there last summer with a bunch of people from school. Picturing that might be good, but I'd have to block out Allie. And then I remembered a dream, I was sitting with a girl on the bluffs. We're on a blanket. Her hand on my back. "Tell me again," she says. . . .

And just like that, I was back to Olivia all over again.

"I don't think swimming is gonna work," I told the doctor.

"Well, you'll find something, a positive thought to 'change the channel' to—does that make sense? It doesn't have to be the same thing every time, and it can be a vague thought, like something about your future—college or what you'd like to eventually do as a career someday. Thinking about things like that might be a good way to move on from the past, and to move forward." She smiled at me so I smiled back to show her I understood what she was saying, but I had already zoned out. I did that a lot lately. Nothing could hold my attention for long. Except thinking about Olivia. For some reason, that was the one thing my mind couldn't let go.

By the middle of my third week at the center, they were talking about transferring me to outpatient. I would only come in four days a week to continue my exercises, but I could live at home again. I was able to get around okay with the leg braces and the special crutches they gave me that hooked onto the top of my arms with a cuff. I almost didn't even need them anymore.

"Your team thinks that it would be okay for us to go

out on a little field trip, maybe out to lunch or to get an ice cream," Mom told me one day when she was visiting. "What do you think?"

I hadn't been anywhere in almost four months, and I wondered whether I was ready to go out in public half crippled. But I said yes, and the next day, Mom arrived to take me out to lunch in town. Navigating into the car with the crutches and leg braces was pretty funny, but once we got to the restaurant, even that was easier. Mom drove about ten miles an hour on the way there. "Mom, I'm not going to break," I had to remind her.

"I know, I know," she said, but I could tell she was nervous having me out of the center.

At the restaurant, it seemed like no one looked twice at us as we stood at the hostess stand. "Two for lunch," Mom said, and they led us to a table where we could look out over the mountains.

"Snow's starting to melt," Mom pointed out. She was right—up at the tops of the mountains, patches of white were disappearing. It was almost April already. School would be out soon, then summer. The lake, hanging out with friends. I wasn't ready to face any of it.

"I was thinking on the way back that we might take a detour," Mom said mischievously. "What would you think of going by Wilson to say hello to all the doctors and nurses there? They would love to see how great you're doing now."

The name of the place made me feel funny—not quite scared, but nervous, anxious. "Do you think it would be okay—I mean, aren't we supposed to get back to rehab?"

"We have the whole afternoon. I told them I was taking you for a haircut, too, but I know you'd rather do anything than that!"

She was right.

After lunch, I stood outside while she pulled the car around and then we headed for Wilson, about twenty minutes away from the rehabilitation center. Mom talked the whole time about how she had some company come out to the house to get it all set up for me next week. Bars in the shower so I could hold myself up, some exercise equipment in the den so I could keep up with my physical therapy on weekends. She was pretty excited about it. I thought about my room, and how long it had been since I had seen it. I was sure it would be the same, but I was returning to it so different. So much had happened since I last slept in that bed. I felt like another person. Another version of West.

The outside of Wilson looked totally unfamiliar to me. I realized I had never actually seen it before. It wasn't what I pictured from the inside, just a low gray building tucked in the foothills with an unassuming sign out front.

When we walked in, a long desk was on our left. I remembered this from my walks in the wheelchair. "I don't think we need to check in; we aren't here to see a patient," Mom explained to the man behind the desk. "Oh hi, Cheryl!" She waved to someone across the hallway, at the nurses' station. "Go on in," the man said, barely looking up.

Mom walked to the station desk and I followed on my crutches. "Oh my God, is this who I think it is?"

When I looked up, I recognized the bitchy nurse, now with a big smile on her face like she was so happy to see me. "So tall and handsome! We miss you around here. Look at him, would you?" She grabbed Mom's arm. "You must be so tickled!"

Her face looked so different, smiling, that I was confused. I almost blurted out something about how she had always been a bitch to me, but thankfully I noticed someone else rounding the corner. Norris.

"Your mom told me you might come by today, so I switched my shift to get to see you." Her huge grin felt like sunshine. "Come over here," she said, pulling me into a hug. When she let go of me, I could see tears in her eyes. "I cannot believe what I am seeing. You didn't get this boy a haircut yet?" she joked to Mom. Norris pushed my hair back from my face.

"You always did that," I said. "You always pushed my hair out of my eyes. . . ."

"Your mom told me that you remembered a lot of your time here, and I just couldn't believe it. Do you actually remember me?" She looked at me so earnestly, I almost laughed.

"I don't know," I scoffed. "You still counting those points?"

"Oh!" She covered her mouth. "Did I . . . ? I must have been complaining! Oh, who knows what else I told you! You poor thing!" She wrapped her arm around my waist and squeezed hard. "He is a tall drink of water, isn't he?" she said to Mom and Nurse Cheryl.

"He's been doing just great, going home next week," Mom told them.

"Well, there is someone else who wants to see you. Mrs. Spencer, do you remember Dr. Yung?" Nurse Cheryl said, coming around the desk.

"I do, and I'd love to see him," Mom said, following her down the hall. "Right back," she said over her shoulder to me and Norris.

Norris didn't say anything, just stood with her arm around me, squeezing.

"Can I see my old room?"

"Oh sure, honey. It's still empty, come on." She led me the other way down the hall, and two doors down on the left, she stopped. "This is it." She flipped the light switch. It was as I remembered. The wall of windows. The green plastic chair by the bed. "All the machines are gone," I pointed out. Just the beds and chair were in the room.

"You do remember it, don't you?" Norris said, looking into my face as if she was searching for something. "It's like a miracle, you know, it is just a miracle."

"Nurse Norris," I heard a woman call from a few doors down. "Could you help me with this cart?" I saw the woman but didn't recognize her; she must not have been assigned to me.

"Stay right here, mister," Norris told me as she moved down the hallway to help the other nurse. They pulled at the cart, trying to reattach a loose wheel without dumping the whole thing over. It was full of medical supplies I recognized—tubes and syringes, bandages and pill bottles. It would be a mess to clean up. I moved a few steps to go to them, automatically, to help if I could, but I stopped when I realized what I was moving toward, where I was standing. The place I didn't want to be. Outside room 203. I was outside her room. But it wasn't her room. Because the girl in my head didn't exist. I made her up. I took my eyes off Norris for just a second and slowly turned my head to the left, terrified of what I might see. There was someone in the bed. There were machines—a ventilator, heart monitor, IV—everything I had around my bed when I was here. Seeing it all sent a sick wave of nausea through me. I never wanted to be in a hospital again.

I took a step into the room, then another, silently on my crutches. I could only see the legs under a neatly tucked blanket. The green curtain around the bed was pulled forward just a little, just enough so that I couldn't see who was there. But I had to see. I knew it wouldn't be her. But I just had to be sure.

I stepped around the curtain and raised my eyes. It was girl. A young girl. With short dark hair and pale skin. I could hear my own heart beating in my ears, pulsing. I forgot to breathe. It was Olivia. But it wasn't. Her hair had been cut. Something had happened to her face. It was softer than I knew it to be; one cheek had a long salmon-colored scar running across it. Her nose was not a straight line anymore, but crooked, off a bit. But she was still beautiful. My Olivia. I moved closer to her, listening to the heart monitor beeping out the rhythm of her body. She was real, and she was alive. I reached forward and touched her small white hand. It was warm.

"West, honey, oh, there you are," Norris whispered. "Come on, that's not it, it's this room here, the empty one." She steered me out of Olivia's room and back into 201.

"What's wrong with that girl?" I asked her quickly.

"Oh, she's been here a while. She's PVS, not like you."

"PVS?"

"Persistent vegetative state," Norris explained, moving a pile of linens to the bottom of the empty bed in my old room. "We all knew you were going to be okay—well, I did. Most folks like you do wake up—some don't do as well as you're doing, but they almost always come back to us."

"And what about her?" I asked, fearing that I already knew the answer.

Norris shook her head. "No, she's got no brain activity. It's real sad, isn't it? That's why I think you are a miracle. You should always remember that, okay?"

Olivia was real. It had happened. But she would never wake up. The girl I met, the girl I fell in love with wasn't alive—she was a ghost. Her body was in the room next door, but she wasn't really here. I would never see Olivia, my Olivia, again.

Chapter 25

When Mom found me, standing in my old room with tears running down my face, she wasn't too happy. "What are you doing in here?" she demanded, looking at Norris.

"I wanted to see it, Mom. I asked her," I told her quickly, wiping my cheeks, before she blamed the nurse.

"I didn't know it would be so upsetting," Norris explained. "I think he's just happy, aren't you?" Norris put her hand on my back.

"It's time to go; they'll be wondering where we are," Mom said curtly. She touched my arm but I pulled away.

Norris could tell that Mom was pissed, but she just stayed calm. "West, anytime you want, you come back and visit me. I usually go on about six in the evening, okay? I mean that, anytime." She winked at me as Mom led me out of the room.

"What were you doing in there?" Mom asked angrily as soon as we were out of earshot.

"What's the big deal?" Inside I felt like my mind was bubbling over, about to explode. But she had no idea what I had just seen, what had just happened to me. How much my life had changed in just the few minutes she wasn't by my side. Part of me wanted to turn her around and show her room 203. Show her Olivia. Show her it was real, it had happened. But the other part of me knew she still wouldn't believe it. Just because the girl looked like the girl I imagined didn't make it real to her. So I knew her name. So I knew how she looked before. Mom would find some way to explain it away. The psychologist would have some new diagnosis. Seeing Olivia didn't change anything for anyone but me. How could they understand? No one would ever understand. No one but Olivia and me.

Mom went on talking: "I just . . . I didn't know where you were." She paused to smile and wave good-bye at the guard at the front desk, then turned back to scold me. "You scared me; I was looking for you."

"Mom, I'm okay!" I practically yelled. "Just drop it. I don't want to talk about it." I just needed her to be quiet for a minute. I needed to think. We walked through the sliding door out the front sidewalk where a woman was standing, smoking.

"Fine. I'll go get the car," Mom said. "Stay here." She looked at me pointedly.

"I won't move." I scowled at her. So much for our first outing. I looked over at the woman to see if she had caught any of our embarrassing fight, and realized that I had seen her before. Dark hair, long coat.

It was Olivia's mom.

"Hello," she said after I'd been staring at her for a few moments. I had forgotten about her beautiful voice, the lilt of her French accent.

"I'm sorry, you just—you look familiar." I shook my head, trying to think of what to say next.

"You're visiting someone?" She motioned toward the doors. When I nodded yes, she went on. "Also me. That's probably why I look familiar." Her smile was so much like Olivia's, it startled me. "How old are you?" she asked, stubbing out her cigarette on the sidewalk with her heel.

"Seventeen."

She nodded. "My daughter is about your age." Her smile was sad.

"Oh." It was on the tip of my tongue to say *I know. I know your daughter*. I could see Mom's car pulling around and into the cul-de-sac. I had to make this quick, and not too obvious. "Is she a patient?"

She nodded. "Two years." I held my breath, hoping she would say more. "When they found her, she wasn't breathing. We don't know how long." She looked down at her gloves for a moment. "Long enough."

"What happened to her?" I asked before I could stop

myself. Part of me didn't want to hear the answer. Part of me already knew what she would say.

She cleared her throat. "She had been, how do you say it? *Violée.* Assaulted."

Olivia didn't have an eating disorder. That's not why she was here. Of course she didn't. She never told me what had happened to her. I never wanted to think too hard about it.

But I knew. Somehow, I had always known.

I was back in the dream. But this time, I wasn't looking at him. At the blood on his hands. I was looking at her. For the first time, I looked down at the girl on the ground. Her white leotard torn and wrenched down in the front, splattered with dark blood. Around her neck a thin pink scarf, tight, cutting into the skin. She's coughing, choking on her own blood.

Mom gave a short honk.

"I believe your ride is here," Olivia's mom said. "It was nice to meet you." She leaned in and I could see that her eyes were exactly the same as Olivia's—same color, same shape, but with small wrinkles around them. "I'm Sophie." She took her glove off and put her hand out to mine.

I hesitated, wondering if I should make up a name, not tell her the truth. "I'm West." I took her hand in mine and felt the same small, strong grip as her daughter's.

"Well, West, until we meet again." I knew Mom was

watching us, so I quickly turned away and headed to the car. Mom got out and put my crutches across the back seat. She watched as Olivia's mom went through the sliding door and back into the hospital.

"Was that one of the other nurses?" Mom asked casually.

"No, just some woman." As we pulled away, I watched out the window until the hospital disappeared on the horizon. It felt like a part of me had been left behind there, and there was no way I could ever get it back.

Mom talked the entire ride; I caught only some of it. "Maybe it wasn't such a good idea . . . you should mention this to your psychologist. . . ." Her words all jumbled together, I didn't care about what she was saying. The sick feeling in my stomach was one of realization. No one— not Mom, not the psychologist, not Norris or Mike or even Olivia's mom was going to be able to help me out of this. No one could understand. No one would believe me. I was alone. But I knew one thing: I wasn't insane. It *had* happened. Olivia was real. And no one was going to take her away from me again.

Chapter 26

The next day, when the psychologist came in for our meeting, I was ready for her. I knew my mom had probably already spoken to her, or the other doctors, and told them about the hospital yesterday, how I had freaked out, cried seeing my old room. They didn't know the whole story, but it didn't really matter. I couldn't hide my reaction yesterday, but now I was ready to explain it away.

On the treadmill that morning, I had walked without using the handrails. Just walking, with braces on, but still. This was progress. And as I thought about what happened yesterday, what I had seen at that hospital, I realized something. No one had been where I had been. No one else—not my parents, my friends, not the doctors, the psychologists—none of them knew what I had been through. What it was like to be in a coma. What things I had seen or done or felt. Who was there with me. They didn't know. And trying to explain it to them would just make them think I was crazy. That I needed help. They would keep me here longer, think that I couldn't cut it at home, or at school. So I needed to act like they wanted me to act. To stop talking about Olivia. To act like I had forgotten all about that. About her. It was the only way to get out of here and get on with what I needed to do. I had made Olivia a promise that I would come back for her, no matter what. I didn't know what that meant, but I had to figure it out. And being stuck in here, or worse yet, in a loony bin, was no way to do that. I resolved to be the most normal, happy, cheerful former coma patient anyone had ever seen. I was going to put a smile on my face and act like everything was grand. That was the only way.

I took a shower and got dressed to sit down with the psychologist. I knew I couldn't be too forced, too happy, but I was ready to say what she needed to hear. And it worked.

"Your mother tells me you had a visit to Wilson Center yesterday. Do you want to talk about that?"

I explained what it was like, the overwhelming emotions I felt at seeing my room. But how happy and grateful I was to be better, to be moving on.

"It can be very emotional to see those other patients

there, the ones who are in a similar situation to what you were in. Do you think it was seeing them that made you feel that way?"

"I didn't really see any other patients," I lied. "It was just the memory of being there, you know, being powerless and hopeless, like we talked about."

"And last night—any dreams? Did that dream about the man attacking someone come back again?"

I shook my head. "Actually, I haven't had that dream since I left Wilson. I guess I only had it there." That was actually the truth, but now I knew why. The dream was connected to Olivia—to her attack, not to Wilson, and not to me. But I wasn't about to tell the doctor that.

"I think you haven't had that dream since your surgery, since you regained the control of your body. When you lost that sense of being powerless, the dream stopped at the same time."

I could tell she was really pleased with herself, with her theory. And actually, I'm sure it was grounded in some psychology truths. But she didn't know the whole story. "Yeah, I hadn't thought about that," I told her, trying to look thoughtful. "That really makes sense." I watched her face to be sure I wasn't laying it on too thick.

We talked a little bit about my mom and her reaction to being at the hospital, and about being with me out for the first time since my accident, and then wrapped up the session. I was relieved she hadn't asked about Olivia at all. "Next week I hear you'll be an outpatient, so I'll only be seeing you once a week, on Wednesday." She watched my face.

"Yeah, I think that sounds good."

"But West, I want you to know that I'm always here for you, and if you feel like you need to talk more than that, we can increase our sessions to twice a week. You can also call me if you find that the transition to home life is harder than you thought. Your mom has my card with my direct line on it. You use it if you need to, okay?"

I nodded and tried to look very serious, but inside I was celebrating. Only once a week, I could do that. I could hold it together.

When I had time to think over the next couple of days—on the treadmill or in bed at night—my mind kept returning to the conversation with Olivia's mom. I would play it back like I was watching a movie; every word she said, every subtle thing, everything I said. That Olivia had been attacked was not actually a surprise to me, I found. It wasn't startling. Somehow I knew it; from the moment she said it, the memory of the dream washed over me and I knew it. It felt like an old memory—like when you smell some type of food and it brings you back to the cafeteria in your kindergarten school. Suddenly you are there, really there; you remember everything—the tile on the floor, what the little table was like, the milk carton in front of you. When her mom said the word *assaulted*, I knew. Yes. But I had always known, I just hadn't wanted to know. Olivia had been hurt, that was clear. Something terrible had happened to her, but she didn't want to talk about it, and I was happy to let it go. I didn't want to think about someone doing that to her. But she showed me, and I saw it instead, in my dreams, even though my brain didn't want to figure it out. Didn't want to put the pieces together. But now that I had, there was no removing that knowledge. My room at Wilson was haunted, but not by a former patient. It was haunted by Olivia, by what had happened to her, by the girl that she was before. I wondered if she even knew. Did she know what had happened to her or was she like me, unwilling to examine it? Not ready to really know?

I wanted to know more about her attacker—had he been caught, did he look exactly like the man in my dreams? I had computer access at the center, and I had used it just a few times. Sometimes they had me practice my typing on the keyboard; I was still a little rusty with the fine motor skills. But I was too paranoid to look up anything about Olivia and her case. What if they could trace the things I was doing on the center's computer? That would have to wait until I was home, where I knew how to clear the search memory quickly and easily, so my parents wouldn't know what I was doing.

Something about knowing the truth made the pattern of my days at the center less of a struggle. I wasn't constantly doubting myself, or worrying. I eased into my schedule and made more progress. I was happier. After weeks of constantly restraining my thoughts, of telling myself that Olivia wasn't real, now I knew she was. When I thought of her, it made me smile. She was real, I knew where she was, and I knew that I could see her again. Maybe not the way I used to, but she was real. And that made all the difference. I had a secret, and something about that was exciting. Like when you have a crush on someone and you feel extra alive for no reason. I felt like that. I had something again—what had been taken away from me was returned. Not the way I thought it would be, but it was better than nothing, than being told the girl I was in love with didn't exist. She did; I had seen her. That was enough to keep me going for now.

When Mike came to visit the day before my release, he noticed the difference. He brought some new tunes and they let us listen to his iPod in a corner of the physical therapy room, even though a few other patients were in there. No one seemed to mind. We played a few rounds of the card game Spit—something that my cognitive therapist had taught me. It was supposed to help with my mental agility, as he called it, and it seemed to be working. "Dang, for somebody with brain damage, you are kicking my ass," Mike joked after I beat him a second time.

"I don't really have brain damage," I explained. "I just have to get used to using my mind again."

"A three-month nap will do that to you." Mike smiled.

"Yeah, it's pretty pathetic that I've been in a coma and I'm still better than you at cards," I pointed out.

"Oh it's *on*, coma boy," Mike said, dealing out the cards for a rematch. At the end of the afternoon, I had won nine times, he had seven, so we were pretty close, but still . . . I was feeling pretty good, and it must have been clear. When Mike was leaving he pulled me in for a bro hug and then hesitated at the door. "Look, not to get all romantic on you or anything, but I'm glad you're back. I'm glad you're like— *you*—again." Mike looked embarrassed.

"Yeah, I am feeling pretty good. You can tell?"

Mike nodded. "When you first woke up, you were scary—like seriously scary—because you'd seem normal, but then you weren't . . . I was worried." His face was serious. "But now, I mean, they're letting you go home, right?"

He looked like he doubted himself, so I had to reassure him. "Tomorrow. I think I'm ready. It's been a long time since I've felt normal, so thanks for noticing."

Mike smiled. "What kind of friend would I be if I didn't warn you when you were acting loco?" He punched my arm as he turned to go. I was glad to see him slip back into his old self. When he got serious, it scared me. "Call me when you're home, I'll come over. I think Xbox will totally help you with that 'fine motor skill' shit you were talking about."

I had to laugh, but he was probably right. The controls for some of those games were pretty complicated. As I watched Mike walk to his car, I realized that I wasn't going to be doing a lot of anything else when I got home. I wasn't going back to school this year, that had already been decided. I would start my junior year over in the fall, a total redo. I was bummed that Mike and Allie would be seniors without me, but the upside was that this would give me a chance to get my grades up. I'd been coasting on a C average, spending more time biking than studying. But that would all be different now.

The next morning, both Mom and Dad came to get me. My room was already packed up, and we went into the therapy room to say good-bye to everyone. I would be back tomorrow for an all-day appointment, so this wasn't really good-bye. Still, it felt sort of significant. The stroke lady gave me a hug, even though she knew she would see me again, probably the next day. "I'm so happy for you," she said, smiling in her lopsided way. I was happy for me too.

"Do you want to stop for lunch?" Dad offered, climbing behind the wheel of Mom's car.

"I kind of just want to get home," I admitted, and Mom gave me a quick smile.

"I can make us sandwiches when we get to the house," she offered. We had my crutches in the trunk, but I didn't really need them anymore. I was able to get by pretty well with just the braces on, though I walked stiffly. They told me I would always be a little tight, because of the fusion in my spine.

When we reached the house, I was surprised to see how unchanged everything was. My room was cleaned up, things put away and the bed made, which I knew I hadn't done, but otherwise the same as I remembered it. I looked over at my laptop sitting on my desk, happy to see it was there, and that I could use it when I got a minute away from my parents.

Mom made lunch and we all sat around the table talking until Dad said he had to go and take a meeting by phone. "I'll just be at the hotel—this shouldn't take long. I was thinking I'd like to take you two out to dinner tonight, if you're up for it?"

Mom and I agreed it sounded good, and we would meet at our favorite Italian restaurant later. Another nice thing to come out of my accident was that Mom and Dad were getting along better than they had in years. Better than I'd ever seen them get along, actually. It was pretty awesome to see them hanging out, I had to admit.

After Dad left, Mom showed me the new equipment she had put in the den. A lot of it was stuff they had in physical therapy, and I was impressed. "This must have cost a bundle," I said, looking at the Pilates Reformer that now took up one side of the room.

"You know what, though," Mom explained, "I'm going to try to use this stuff too. Why not, right? I should get into shape as well." I wondered when, between her job and schlepping me back and forth to physical therapy, she was going to have the time, but then I realized she was just trying to make me feel better about the expense she had gone to. "Do you want to watch some TV, or rest . . . ?"

"I think I'll go lie down, if that's okay," I told her. "I feel okay; I just want to take a nap if we're going out tonight."

Mom smiled. "No headaches or anything though?"

I shook my head. This was something the doctor had told us both to be on the lookout for, but so far my head had been feeling fine. I went into my room and closed the door behind me. I couldn't believe how good it felt to sit on my own bed, in my own room, with my laptop. I took a deep breath and started doing some research online, typing as quietly as I could so that Mom wouldn't hear me.

It took a while to find the report of Olivia's attack. I hadn't realized that they don't release the names of minors, so searching for her name got me nowhere. I finally found something about a fifteen-year-old female victim by searching with the key word "coma." It had happened in the city, two years ago, downtown. "The victim, a fifteen-year-old female, remains comatose at St. Joseph's Hospital," one article said. This must have been before she was moved to Wilson. There weren't many details available. A young girl had been attacked; she was not breathing when she was discovered by a bus driver. The next day, a twenty-seven-year-old suspect had been arrested, but his name was not released. An article a few days later listed the victim as stabilized in a coma. This one had the attacker's name because he had been charged with the crime: Thomas Mason. Once I found his name, it was easy to find his sentencing papers, and where he was serving his time.

So he was real, an actual person. Not just someone from my dreams. A real man, sitting in a prison. I tried to picture him, what he was doing right now.

"West, sweetie, you okay in there?" Mom knocked gently on the door. I glanced at the clock, surprised to see that I'd been in my room for two hours.

"Yup, fine, just waking up. I'll be right out." The sun was starting to set outside, and I knew we'd be meeting Dad soon for dinner. But I had what I needed. I hadn't found any photos of this guy online, but I knew where he was, and that was a start.

Chapter 27

My days fell into a pattern, with Mom dropping me off at the rehabilitation center before work and picking me up in the afternoon. She had arranged her work schedule so that she could make the half-hour drive there and back each day, but it meant that she had to do all her paperwork at home, sitting at the dining room table at night. It made me feel pretty crappy knowing how much I had already disrupted her life with everything that was going on with me. "You know, Mike said he could pick me up one of these days, save you the return trip," I offered.

Mom laughed. "Are you kidding with me? You are not getting into a car with Mike, especially not to go to physical therapy. I mean, seriously . . ."

I wasn't allowed to drive yet, which presented a real

problem. There was somewhere I wanted to go, someone I wanted to see, and I didn't know how I was going to get there. Friday was my only day off from the center, and I was supposed to just rest at home. I knew if I asked, Mom would say no to hanging out with Mike if it meant going in his car anywhere. She felt I was still too fragile. I wondered if she would ever trust me to be out on my own again. I knew she came in to check on me two or three times a night sometimes, like she did when I was little and I had a fever.

The first Friday came and Mom actually stayed home from work. We went out to lunch, and then she insisted I get a haircut at her place. I had to agree—my hair had passed from long and sort of cool-looking to dirty and hippie. Mom told the stylist I wanted just a trim, but I actually wanted it shorter. I directed the lady as she moved around the chair, even having her buzz the back pretty short. I could tell Mom was happy with the results, and so was I. The haircut was perfect for something I had in mind for the next week.

That weekend, Mike and Allie came over for dinner on Saturday night—Mom ordered a pizza but generally stayed out of our way. We played some Xbox and then watched a DVD Mike brought over. "Really, who thought this was a good idea?" Allie asked, holding up the case. It showed two teenagers, a girl and boy, running down a dark street from some ominous shape behind them.

"What?" Mike said. "You don't approve?"

"*Two teens get more than they bargained for when they accept a ride from a stranger,*" Allie read off the case. "*They soon find themselves in a real-life game of cat and mouse with an evil force . . .* forget it, I'm not watching this."

Allie and I were in sort of a new place. Not boyfriend and girlfriend, that was for sure. But not exactly just friends either. When we had been broken up before, we didn't hang out, we didn't speak at all. But this time, everything was different. I understood that whatever romance had been between us was gone, but sometimes, like while watching her face when she was reading the description of the movie, I would get this hurt in my chest and an uncontrollable urge to grab her around the waist, squeeze her, tickle her, be the way we used to be. Close. But then the memory of everything that had happened would wash over me, and the feeling would pass. I knew that what I really craved was that contact, to be close to someone, the girl I loved, but that girl wasn't Allie. I didn't want Allie that way anymore, and I didn't think I ever would again.

Even though Allie said she was leaving the second we put the movie on, somehow we convinced her to hang out for part of it. She had to be home early, and I got the feeling she was happy to leave about twenty minutes into the movie—she was watching it behind her hands most of the time anyhow. Mike was staying over.

When the movie was done, Mom set up the guest

room for Mike but he hung in my room pretty late, just talking. There was something I'd been meaning to ask him, a favor, but I didn't want anyone else to know about it, so I waited until I knew Mom was asleep. "Can you drive me somewhere next Friday?"

"Sure," Mike said. "No problem. I'll pick you up after I get out of school."

"That's the thing, it needs to be during the day, so . . ." I hated to ask Mike to skip school to be my chauffeur, but he was the only person I could trust.

"Where do you need to go? To do your workout?" Mike acted out lifting some weights—he liked to tease me about physical therapy, claiming that I was just trying to bulk up now. He called it "hitting the gym" and was always asking to see my arm muscles.

"No, I need to go and see someone."

"Okay," Mike said. "But you're going to need to tell me where if I'm driving you. I mean, unless you think I can drive blindfolded."

"It's going to sound weird, and I can't really explain it all to you, but . . . I need to see someone who's in prison."

Mike looked like he was trying to process what I had just said. "You know someone in prison?"

"No, I don't know him. Look, I can't tell you more. I know it sounds weird. And I know I'm asking a big favor, but this is just something I need to do. Are you in or not? I'll pay for gas."

Mike thought about it for a second. "You know, every time I think you're back to your old self, you do something so freaky. . . ." He shook his head. "I don't know about this."

"I'll explain everything later," I told him. But deep down, I knew I probably never would. "I just need to check something out. Then I can tell you more."

"You're sure you're okay, like, your brain and everything? This isn't some delusion or whatever, like you had before?"

I sat staring at him for a second, and I almost opened my mouth to tell him the truth. I wanted to tell someone— about Olivia, about the fact that she was real, about the dreams I'd had, about Thomas Mason. But Mike looked so worried, I knew if I shared it all with him now, he would think I was insane. He would probably end up telling my mom, and then I'd be back where I started.

"I'm okay," I assured him. "Really. It's just that, I'm trying to start over here, get back on track. Does that make sense?"

It seemed to be enough of an explanation for Mike. "Is this, like, a relative or someone you never told me about?"

I nodded. "Something like that, yeah, I'm just—I'm not sure I'm ready to tell everyone about it yet. Okay?"

"I think I get it." Mike got up off my bed. "Yeah, shit, I'll do it. Of course."

"Thanks, this is important to me and I've got no one else to ask."

He gave me a close look and I tried my best not to

appear overly anxious or crazy, just normal. "Okay, I'll see you in the morning." He left and closed the door quietly behind him.

In the morning, while Mom made pancakes, we were back to our regular selves, joking around at the kitchen table. "You should slow down on the carbs," Mike pointed out as I took my third plate of pancakes. "Seriously, you're looking a little puffy."

I looked down at my baggy jeans and loose T-shirt. You could still count every rib. "Maybe I should go back on the liquid diet?" I joked.

Mike gave me a serious nod as he shoved a huge bite of syrup-covered pancakes in his mouth.

"Boys, I don't like that talk even as a joke," Mom cut in, putting some more hot pancakes on the table between us. "In fact, I'm getting you a glass of milk," she said, moving to the fridge. "Mike, would you like one?"

Mike just rolled his eyes at me. I guess I had done a good job convincing him that I was okay, and that this favor was something I needed to do to move on. I just needed to be sure. When he left that morning, we made a plan to hang out midweek, after school on Wednesday, so I knew everything was cool.

———

On Friday morning, we started out early, right after Mom left for work. Just in case something crazy happened, and she got home before us, I left her a note explaining that I'd gone over to Mike's after school let out. Hopefully, though, she would stay at work all afternoon like she'd said she was going to do.

I had printed out directions to the prison, which was almost an hour away. Mike came prepared with snacks and a new mix of tunes. If I hadn't been anxious about where were going, it actually would have been a fun road trip. I noticed that Mike talked about everything but where we were headed, and why, as he drove along the highway. Mike mentioned a party at Cindy's house this weekend. "It's tomorrow, do you think . . . ?" He gave me a skeptical look, knowing that my mom had been treating me like a five-year-old lately.

I shook my head. With all the medications I was taking, I couldn't drink. Not that it held any interest for me. Escaping from reality was not a priority right now—I felt like I just returned to it. "Yeah, not this weekend. If I get caught today, I might be grounded for a while anyhow," I joked.

As we got closer to the exit we'd need to take, Mike got quieter, less animated. His hands were tight on the steering wheel and he looked tense, leaning forward in his seat. "So, uh, how long do you think you're going to be in there?" he finally asked.

"Not long," I said. From what I'd read online about the

prison, weekday visiting was pretty light. On weekends, it could take hours to get through because that's when everyone came. We drove up to the visitor's gate and a guard leaned out, startling us both. "Hello, gentlemen, can I help you?"

Mike looked to me, terrified. I leaned over him to answer the guard. "We're here to . . . visit someone," I said quickly, hearing my voice go up. I sounded like a scared little kid.

"Have you been here before?" the guard asked.

Both Mike and I shook our heads. "Park in lot B, enter through the south gate." He pointed toward a huge parking lot just inside the fence.

"Thank you," Mike said politely, and put the car back into gear. Just then, my cell rang: Mom. I had to tell her quickly that I was fine and everything was okay. Not a lie, but I also didn't mention that I wasn't at home or where I was. "I'm probably going to be at the office until about two or so, then I'm showing a house—do you think you'll be okay until then?"

I told her she could work later if she wanted to, that I was absolutely great and actually enjoying the alone time, which I think made her feel better. "Then I'll see you for dinner tonight," she said cautiously. "But you call me if anything comes up."

Mike peered out at the prison through the windshield.

"Please tell me that you don't need me to come in there with you."

"No, you can hang here. I really won't be that long." I checked to be sure I had Thomas Mason's prison ID number and my wallet in my back pocket before I got out. "See you in a few," I told Mike. He looked terrified, like just being this close to the prison meant you were about to get arrested. He was probably just thinking about the underage drinking he had done and gotten away with—not to mention other illegal stuff.

"Hey, where are your leg things?" Mike noticed as I climbed out of the car that I had left the bulky braces at home. I barely needed them anymore.

"I'm supposed to take a day off now and then," I lied. "Something about making my muscles stabilize on their own."

Mike pulled his sleeve up and made a muscle with his arm. "Stabilize this," he joked. But I could tell he was nervous. When I reached the entrance door to the prison, I turned to see him looking down at his phone in the car. He would be fine.

There was a line of people inside waiting and I joined it, trying to look calm and also trying to look older. You had to be eighteen to visit someone in prison without a guardian, and I wasn't. I had my fake ID with me—the one that now said I was twenty-two years old. It might be good enough to fool the cashier at 7-11, but I wasn't sure it was going to cut it here. The photo wasn't even me—it was some guy who had gone to my high school a few years before, repeated senior year, and now worked at the Best Buy in town. He had made a little business of occasionally "losing" his license and getting a new one. I was one of a few fake Derek Mitchells in our town. His hair was short, buzzed in the back, just like mine was now, and about the same color. I hoped it would be good enough.

When I got to the front of the line, the guy behind the window asked me who I was there to see. I passed him the piece of paper with the name and ID number on it. "Sign in," he slid me a clipboard with a sheet of paper on it. I signed the name Derek Mitchell and slid it back to him. "ID," the guy said. I took my fake out of my wallet and pushed it over to him. I could feel sweat forming on my forehead but I didn't dare wipe it off. The guy looked at the license and, without ever looking up at me, slid it back. "They'll call you from the waiting room," he said. I followed where I had seen other people before me in line go, into a small room off the main entrance with a sign outside that read HOLDING.

The room had rows of plastic seats and I took one, looking around at the other folks who were there with me. They were mostly women—young, like girlfriends, and older, like moms. There was only one other guy, and he looked like someone's grandfather. I wondered about who they were here to see. Husbands, boyfriends. Sons. The thought sent a shudder down my spine. Thomas Mason was someone's son. There might be a woman in here who was visiting him. A girlfriend. A wife? I blocked the thought from my mind. Who could marry a guy like that? Who would ever want to be with him, after what he had done? Then I stopped myself. What if he wasn't the guy—the one I had been having dreams about? I was pretty sure he would be, but I hadn't really prepared myself for the chance that my dreams had been just that: dreams.

I put my ID back into my wallet and noticed that my hands were shaking. What was I doing here? This had seemed like a good idea—like something that I had to do—when I was looking up Olivia's case. But now that I was here, sitting in this prison, waiting to see this guy, I felt like I had made a disastrous mistake. I could get up and walk out—I didn't have to do this. But I knew I wouldn't. As scary as it was, I needed to see him. I just needed to be sure, for myself, for Olivia. If he was who I thought he was, then it was real. Then Olivia and I *had* been together, in some place that no one else could understand or touch. It was proof. Because there was no way I could have ever seen this guy before, known what he had done to her, what he looked like. It was impossible. Unless Olivia had shown it to me.

"Mitchell for T. Mason," the guard called out. "Mitchell for T. Mason."

It took me a moment to register that I was the "Mitchell" he was looking for, and I stood on shaky legs and made my way to the door on the opposite side of the room. The guard led me through to a long, narrow room with a piece of glass running down the middle. There were small booths set up on either side of the glass, like library cubicles with chairs, and each had their own phone attached. It was exactly like I had seen on TV shows, and that was comforting for some reason.

The guard pointed vaguely down to the end of the row of cubicles and checked something off on his clipboard. "You've got twenty," he said to me as I moved passed him.

"Yeah, thanks," I murmured, trying to act like I did this every day. I stepped slowly to the space he had pointed out, but somehow I already knew what I would see.

The long, dirty hair, wild eyes, and pockmarked face. I knew it well. I knew it would be him.

And it was. But the hair was gone, now replaced with a crew cut. The skin was raw and broken out. Even though he had to be thirty now, his skin looked like a teenager's. And his eyes were the same. Maybe worse than I remembered.

I pulled out the plastic chair and took a seat. As he reached for the phone, I noticed the small tattoos on his hands, letters, something written in the space between his thumb and first finger, and a cobweb over the back of his hand. I pictured those hands around Olivia's neck. I picked up my phone and held it to my ear.

"Who the hell are you?"

I was surprised that I had never thought about what this would be like, to actually have a conversation with him. For some reason, I had only imagined seeing him, confirming what I already knew. "I'm a friend. A friend of Olivia Kemple's," I said.

It took him a minute to register who I was talking about. Then his face took on a harder look. "And? What do you want, a medal or something?"

"I just wanted to see you," I told him honestly.

"Well, now you've seen me. Happy?" He leaned back in his chair and stared at me. I didn't know what to say. "How is she, still got a pulse?"

I swallowed hard, feeling like I might throw up. "Yeah," I said weakly. "She's in a coma, it's stage one." I didn't know why I added that, like he would know what it meant, or even care.

His face took on a softer look. "But she's alive, right?"

"Yeah, she's alive," I said, my voice catching on the word. I held the phone tighter to keep my hand from shaking. Maybe he did care. Maybe he felt bad about what he had done to her. I wanted to believe that he did. But looking at his face, at his cold eyes, made me doubt that. It didn't matter. I didn't want to think about what it was like for him. I hated him.

We sat staring at each other for a moment, neither of us saying anything. Then he broke the silence. "So what do you want? You want me to say something? You want me to say I'm sorry? You come here to make me feel bad?"

I couldn't answer him. What did I want him to say—was there anything he could say that would make me feel better? This was the man who had hurt Olivia. I was seeing him for real—just a few feet from him, the man who had haunted my dreams for months. But he had no way of knowing that.

Suddenly he slammed his fist on the glass separating us. "Hey, I asked you a question! What do you want?"

I stared at his hand on the glass. But I saw it coming down, over and over again, on her. The sickening sound his fist made when it connected with her skin. When I glanced back up, his face was the angry mask it had been in my dreams.

"Don't touch the glass," I heard one of the guards behind him say.

"You're a waste of time," he hissed at me. He slammed the phone into its holder and pushed his chair back hard. I watched as he left the room through a door in the back, led by a guard back to wherever they were keeping him.

For just a moment, I thought my arms wouldn't move,

that I would be paralyzed again, strapped down, like I was so many times when I saw him in my dreams. That I would be powerless. But I wasn't. I carefully put the phone back into the cradle and sat for a minute thinking about what he had said. A waste of time. That's what he thought of me. That's what he said about Olivia.

I looked down at my hands in front of me on the desk. I made two fists, then opened them, spread my fingers. I was awake. This wasn't a dream.

I walked slowly out through the holding room, and back out into the parking lot. The sun felt good on my face. I stood for a moment on the walkway and just soaked it in, taking a deep breath. I felt like something had been washed off me. Some weight had been lifted. I understood now. What Olivia had shown me and why—all the things she couldn't tell me. I had to see for myself.

So it was real. He was real. Thomas Mason. The things I saw in the hospital—they happened. I thought of the little girl in my room, dripping blood, opening the drawer. That wasn't a dream. And the guy with the burned face. He was real too. They had been patients at Wilson, like me, like Olivia. They were still there, in some limbo, the place where I had once been. Where Olivia was now, where I had left her. Unable to get out, to ever leave.

"That was fast." Mike looked up from his phone when I opened the car door. "Did you get to see . . . your mystery prisoner?" I could tell he was trying to keep things light, but I wasn't in any position to help out.

"Yeah, I saw him." I snapped on my seat belt and leaned back. I looked over at Mike, but he was staring out at the prison. I could tell there was something he wanted to say. When Mike got serious, sometimes it took him a minute. I was quiet until he was ready to talk.

"Is this about that girl, the one you thought you knew at the hospital?" he finally said, still not meeting my eyes.

"Sort of," I started to explain. "But it's not what you think. I'm not crazy or anything. I'm okay, I really am." Mike looked over at me, and I could see the worry on his face. I hated what I was putting my friend through. "Trust me."

He started the car and we drove home in silence, broken only when he dropped me off in front of my house. It was late afternoon, but I was happy to see that Mom's car wasn't in the driveway yet.

"Just tell me one thing." I could hear the frustration in Mike's voice. "Did you do whatever it was you had to do?"

"I'll never go back there again," I told him. I thought about Thomas Mason, his fist on the glass. On her. I felt sick to my stomach.

I closed the door to his car and walked up the steps to my house, hearing him drive away as I put the key into the lock. I barely got inside before I raced to the kitchen and retched into the sink. I realized that I had hardly eaten all day as I dry heaved over the counter, feeling like my insides were coming out. When I could catch my breath, I found my note to Mom sitting on the table, the one from this morning. I looked at the words I had written just hours ago and wondered, if I could go back and do this day over again, would I do it differently? Would I decide not to go to the prison? No. There was no other way. I had to see for myself, to know for sure. But now that I knew, I didn't feel better. I felt worse.

I tore the note in half, hard, harder, over and over again until it was nothing but pieces of confetti. Then I sat on the kitchen floor and watched the room get dark, until the sweep of Mom's headlights in the driveway brought me back to the world of the living.

Chapter 28

I had to see Olivia, to talk to her. Now that I knew that my dreams had not been dreams, there was something I needed to tell her. Now that I knew more about her. About the other visions I had while at the hospital. But getting to Wilson was going to be a problem. I couldn't ask Mike, and Allie was also out of the question. Mom was a no. I pulled up the bus-system map on my laptop, but something about taking a bus, or a series of buses to see Olivia felt wrong—I just kept thinking about her waiting at the bus stop that night. Then I started thinking about her spending her days—every day since I had left the hospital—waiting for me to come back, thinking that I had left her and forgotten about her. Alone and haunted by those thoughts, those memories she had shown me. Alone with the others, that little girl, with the man with his burned face. I had to shake my head to make the images go away. I called the cab company and ordered a pick-up for the next day I had off from rehab, after Mom would be gone at work. It would cost a small fortune, but I didn't know how else to get there, and I had to see her.

When the cab pulled up outside, I left my crutches by the door and grabbed my keys. My hands felt damp with sweat as I climbed into the backseat. I told the driver, a gray-haired guy with a beard, where I was headed, and the address, but he just grunted out an "Okay" and started driving. I felt nervous, like I was meeting Olivia for a date or something, butterflies in my stomach. I knew what I had to do once I got there, what I had to say.

"You want me to wait?" the cab driver said when he pulled up outside the Wilson Center.

"I'll probably just call another cab for the way back; I don't know how long I'm going to be," I told him.

"I was going to grab a coffee. I'll swing back by here when I'm done," he said, turning around to look at me. "Off the clock."

I couldn't believe he was being so nice to me. "Um, thanks, that would actually be great."

He grabbed a clipboard next to his seat and starting writing something down as I took out my wallet to pay. "You know somebody in there?" he said, not looking up from his pad.

I swallowed hard. "I do," I said finally. "A friend." The

word caught in my throat. She wasn't a friend. She was so much more. How could I describe what Olivia was to me?

He nodded and looked up at me, waving away my twenty-dollar bill. "I'll be here when you get out, kid." Obviously he knew what kind of patients they had at Wilson. I didn't want to ask how.

I walked in through the sliding door and to the front desk, where I signed in just using an unreadable scribble. You didn't have to say who you were visiting or show ID, so I didn't. The guy behind the desk didn't even look up at me. I walked by the nurses' station confidently, like I came here all the time. No one recognized me, no one noticed me. Why would they? Norris wouldn't be here until the night shift. And without the crutches, with my short hair, I looked nothing like the guy who had been a patient here. I was just another visitor now.

I went down the hall without even looking into my old room. It was dark, and looked like it was still empty anyhow.

"West."

I heard someone say my name, quietly.

I stopped. No, it was impossible.

The voice was so familiar, so linked to this place, for a moment the wires got crossed in my mind and I spun around expecting to see her, to see Olivia standing there. By the time I had turned, I knew it wasn't her, instead it was another face I knew well, a warm, open face.

Nurse Norris.

"West," she said again. "I thought that was you." She put down the chart she was holding and moved closer to me. How the dynamic had changed. Instead of looking down over me, now she stood smiling in front of me, almost a foot shorter than I was. "What a nice surprise."

"I just . . . I just came for a visit," I started to say.

"But not to visit me—I don't usually work days. But you know that already, you remember my schedule." Her eyes held mine and I could tell she was waiting for me to say something. "So what are you doing here?"

I was caught, with no explanation. "I don't know," I finally said. And it wasn't a lie. I was confused. Why was I here? What had I hoped to accomplish? To tell Olivia something, to tell her that it was all real, that the things we had seen and felt were real. That I had seen the man from my dreams, that I understood now. That I had come back for her, like I said I would.

"Come have a seat." Nurse Norris motioned to the chairs off to the side of the hallway and I took one beside her. She waited silently, patiently for me to talk.

"I feel like I knew—" I stopped myself. "Like I know the people here."

"Well of course—you know me." Norris smiled. "But why do I get the feeling you aren't talking about the nurses and the doctors?"

I met her eyes and saw that she understood, or was trying to.

Maybe Norris was the one person in all of this who would understand. Who would believe me. The words rolled out of me, before I could stop myself. "There was a patient here, in my room before me, a man, his face was burned. . . ."

I heard Nurse Norris suck in her breath in shock. I glanced at her and saw her hand go to her heart. "No," she said quietly.

"I saw him. He was standing in my room. His name is Paul."

Norris shook her head, then looked down the hallway. "I can't comment on other patients," she started to say.

"You don't have to say anything; I already know. And there was a girl, a little girl, dripping wet, and blood . . ."

I saw Norris's eyes well up with tears. "Katie," she whispered, biting on her lower lip.

"Yes." I didn't want to tell Nurse Norris how the girl searched the drawer, looking for something. How angry she seemed, how sad. "They're dead, aren't they?" I asked her. But I already knew the answer. Or I thought I did.

Nurse Norris stood up and held her hand out to me. There was a weak smile on her face. "There's something I want to show you."

I stood and took her hand, and let her lead me down the hallway like a child. She stopped outside a room on the other side of the hall and motioned for me to go inside. I looked at the body on the bed, terrified of what I might see.

"This is Paul," she said quietly. He looked different than I remembered, than the photos, than the man who stood in my room that night. The scars on his face were pink now, not blackened and burned. Some hair had grown back around his head, but he was still badly damaged—he had a breathing tube in his throat and a bandage taped over one eye.

"He was in room 201 for a time. He needed some surgery, skin grafting to prevent infection. He was in another hospital, and when he returned he was placed in this room. But he's not dead."

She took my hand and led me from his room before my mind could even process what I was seeing.

"And here's Katie," she said, taking me into an open doorway across the hall. She pulled back the curtain around the bed to reveal a little girl—not dripping with blood, but with carefully braided hair along either side of her face. She looked peaceful, as if she was just sleeping, except the fact that she was also on a respirator and connected to all the beeping, ticking machines beside her bed. It was the little girl I remembered, the one who searched the drawers, who grabbed my arm.

"She's been here for a year now," Nurse Norris explained. "She just turned nine."

"They're all—"

Norris interrupted me, "They're not dead. They're coma patients. Like you were." She paused for a moment, letting me take it in. "Is there anyone else you'd like to see?" Nurse Norris looked down the hall, to the doorway of Room 203. She knew.

"Olivia." I said her name quietly, and something in my voice must have given me away.

"Oh, honey." Nurse Norris put her arms around me and pulled me into her for a hug.

"You believe me? You believe that I saw them?"

"I do." She nodded, but stopped herself. "Why would you want to come back here and surround yourself with so much darkness? Why don't you just leave this all behind you, go on with your life—"

"I can't," I interrupted her. "I can't just forget what I saw. And Olivia, she's still there—she's still stuck there. How do I just walk away knowing that?"

Norris was silent for a moment. "I don't know." She took a deep breath. "I learned a hard lesson when I came to work here. When I first started out, I thought I could save everybody. I thought with enough kindness, with enough attention, maybe . . ." She shook her head. "But most of these patients, they won't get better. That's hard. It's hard to come to work every day and to know that, to keep going, keep caring, when you know how it will end, every time, that the patients you take care of for years will never get better."

She looked at my face to be sure I was following her. "It's just hard, West, and I wish you didn't have to know about it."

I looked down at my sneakers. I felt empty inside, hollow. I thought maybe Nurse Norris would have an answer. The fact that she believed me—that she confirmed what I already knew—was important, but yet it had gotten me nowhere. The people I thought were ghosts haunting the hospital weren't ghosts at all. They were alive, or some version of being alive. They were trapped between being living and being somewhere else. And they were all so deeply unhappy, so sad, lost.

"Why don't you sit with Olivia for a while?" Nurse Norris asked, pulling me from my thoughts. I nodded and she patted the back of my hand. "I think she'd like that," she said, and motioned toward room 203. My knees almost buckled as I moved to walk down the hall; I had forgotten that I'd left my braces at home. Nurse Norris helped me get my balance.

"Come say good-bye before you head out, okay?" She squeezed my arm as I walked down the hall.

When I rounded the doorway to 203, for a split second I expected to see Olivia, my Olivia, sitting in bed, looking up from a magazine, her long hair down around her shoulders, surprised and happy to see me, a smile slowly crossing her face. But she looked exactly as she had the last time; a body in a bed, her dark hair short, the long, deep pink scar across one cheek. I hardly saw those things, though. I knew the girl in the bed wasn't her, wasn't where she was or how she really looked.

I pulled up a chair alongside the bed and took her hand. "It's West," I whispered. "Olivia, it's me." I listened to the sound of the ventilator pushing air into her body, over and over again. The rhythmic, muted beep of the heart monitor.

You have to come back for me.

I thought about how she didn't want me to leave, how hard she tried to convince me not to have the surgery. How scared she was for me.

Don't leave me here.

But how much did she know? Did she understand that waking up would take me away from her, away from wherever we were together? Maybe she was terrified of being alone.

Promise me you'll come back for me.

Or maybe she knew there was only one way out. It was a place you didn't come back from. She had seen others go there before me.

Sometimes I think I'm never going to get out of here.

She was waiting for me to come back. And here I was.

I pulled my chair closer to the bed and put her hand up to my cheek and felt her warmth. "Olivia," I whispered, "I came back for you. Just like you wanted me to." I took a deep breath. "The things we saw, the things we felt, it's all real." I stopped and leaned in, putting my face close to hers. "Those people—the dreams I had. They aren't dreams. Or ghosts. They're real people, but they're stuck here. They can't move on, can't let go."

I glanced at the machine next to the bed that registered her heartbeat, and it stayed rhythmic and calm.

She was one of them. And she didn't know it.

She didn't know that she wasn't going to get better. That's what they were all waiting for. Paul. The little girl, Katie. Olivia. Me, when I was there. We all wanted to live again. But some of us were never going to make it back. I had been lucky.

"I don't want you to be like them." I laid my head on her shoulder and listened to the sound of her heart beating. I hoped she could hear me, could understand me. Minutes passed as we sat quietly like that, listening to the sounds of her body still working, being kept alive. We were together, both of us, in this room. Our bodies were here. But I knew that part of her wasn't here. And it never would be.

I looked at the wires to the machines, plugged into the wall, and into each other. It wouldn't take much to show her I had kept my promise. That I had come back for her.

I realized what Olivia had taught me; she had shown me how to disconnect the ventilator without setting off alarms, without signaling the nurses. She had known all about the feeding tube, the IV. How to disconnect the shunt so no one would know. It would be hours before they noticed. She knew their schedule, and I did, too. Why did she show me those things, unless she wanted me to use that knowledge?

I thought about the steps I would need to go through. I could do it. If that's what she wanted.

"Olivia." I looked at her face. "I can get you out of here. Tell me if that's what you want, and I'll do it." I studied her, waiting for a sign. "Blink once for yes, like you taught me."

Her face remained calm and beautiful, silent. "Blink," I begged. "Please, Olivia, show me that you understand." I sat watching her, but there was no change. "I can't leave you like this, with the rest of them. You don't belong here."

"Oh—" a voice said suddenly behind me, and I jerked away from Olivia, spinning around to see a young nurse pushing a cart into the room. "I didn't know Ms. Kemple had a visitor. So nice to see a friend here." The nurse smiled.

I looked back at Olivia's face, but it was unchanged. The way the nurse talked to her made me sick, that cloying baby talk. I wanted to shake Olivia, to make her understand. To make her answer me. Did she know I was here at all?

I grabbed my coat and stood to leave.

"Don't go on my account . . . ," the nurse started to say,

but I left the room without a backward glance. I couldn't sit there and stare at Olivia—at that girl in the bed—any longer. Coming here had been a mistake. I couldn't help her; I couldn't help any of them. I had failed. I had let her down. I walked by the nurses' station on my way to the doors. Norris was there, doing some paperwork. I looked at her silently, and she nodded.

"You call me anytime. Your mom has my number. I mean that, anytime at all," she said. I gave her a weak smile and moved to the door before she could stand up. I didn't want to drag it out—I didn't want another hug from her, or a long good-bye. I just wanted to get out of the dimly lit hallway, the open door to room 203, the sounds of machines clicking and beeping, keeping all these people alive.

When I stepped outside, I saw the cab waiting for me. I opened the back door and climbed in. The driver was staring out the windshield to the mountains on the horizon. "Snow's melting," he said without looking back at me. I looked up and saw that he was right. The soft white snowcaps that I had seen from my hospital window for all those months were now gone, replaced with the sharp black mountain range that formed the familiar skyline for the city. He slipped the car into gear without even asking where I wanted to go. I guess he assumed I was ready to go home, and I was. He didn't try to make conversation on the drive back, and I was grateful for the silence.

When we got back to my house, I again pulled out my wallet to pay, noticing for the first time that the electronic taximeter was black—he hadn't turned it on. "Save your money, kid," he said, taking a sip of his coffee. "I hope your friend gets out of that place soon."

I opened the back door. "Me too," I whispered, my voice breaking. "Me too."

Chapter 29

I'm holding her hand, warm and small in mine. She looks the same, the girl I knew: her hair is long and dark and swirls around her face and the white pillow. "I've never had a friend that I could trust like you, West. You said you would come back for me, and you did." She smiles, and her face takes on a warm light. "I had never been in love before I met you," she says quietly. "You showed me. You showed me what love is." Her eyes meet mine. "Thank you, West." Such a small thing to say—thank you—but I feel her words wash over me and I'm overwhelmed. It's all okay. I didn't let her down. I came back for her. She knows I'm here. She's not trapped in that dark place anymore, with the rest of them. She's with me, safe.

"I'm so tired. Will you stay with me? Just stay with me

until I'm asleep." Her eyes are closed, her face calm. There are no scars; she's whole again. I look to the machine next to the bed and see that it is slowly winding down, as if I am willing it to. I want it to stop. The beeping becomes slower and slower, then fades altogether. The ventilator stops pumping. The room is quiet; we are alone. "I'm here, Olivia," I tell her. I know that she can hear me. She's free. I stay with her like that as the room grows dark around us. "I won't leave," I whisper to her. "I won't ever leave you."

———

The call came three days later. Mom was in the kitchen putting groceries away when the phone rang. I heard her say, "It's so nice to hear your voice," and then she went on to tell whoever was calling about how well I was doing. When I walked into the kitchen, Mom mouthed to me, "Nurse Norris," and pointed at the phone. I shook my head. I wasn't ready to talk to her, not yet.

"He's in the shower right now, but I'll have him give you a call later, or tomorrow," Mom said, getting off the phone. "Why didn't you want to speak to her? It's so nice of her to call and check up on you, don't you think? She always was my favorite nurse." Mom turned to put something in the fridge and I was relieved she couldn't see my face. She had no way of knowing that I just been at Wilson two days before, and obviously Norris had kept my secret for me.

"Yeah, she was my favorite too."

"You should give her a call tomorrow," Mom said, washing her hands at the sink. "Now, what should we have for dinner?"

———

I knew I wasn't going to call Norris, not tomorrow, not ever. What would I say? I had been haunted by a dream since my visit to Wilson. I couldn't stop thinking about Olivia being there, being trapped there. About all of them. I didn't know how I was going to move on while she was still there. It seemed impossible. But I didn't know what else to do. I had promised Olivia I would be there for her. I wanted to keep my promise, but I didn't know exactly what that meant. And it was killing me.

The next day when my cell rang and flashed "unknown caller," I picked it up without thinking. I just assumed it was my physical therapist, who usually called around that time to set up our schedule. But it wasn't.

"West, it's Nurse Norris. I tried you last night, but you weren't available," she said.

"Oh yeah, Mom told me. I'm sorry, I've just been busy. . . ."

"That's good. I'm happy to hear that you're busy, that you've been getting back to your life," Norris said.

I took a deep breath. I didn't know what to say to her.

"West, I'm calling with some difficult news for you. Do you feel like you're ready to hear it?"

Suddenly I felt a cold wave wash over me. I wanted to hang up on her, to pretend the call had never come. But that wouldn't stop it from being true. "You can tell me."

"It's the patient from room 203, Olivia Kemple. I'm sorry to tell you that she passed. It was early yesterday morning."

I swallowed hard but said nothing.

"Unfortunately she suffered heart failure. There was nothing we could do. It's not uncommon to have organ failure in a long-term coma patient."

I was silent.

"West, are you there?"

"I'm here," I answered.

"If you would like, I can get you the information about the memorial that her mother is planning. If you want to go. I'll be there."

I paused, trying to take in what she was telling me. Olivia was gone. The girl at Wilson, the body in the bed. She wasn't being kept alive there anymore. My Olivia.

"West, I'll be going, if you want to come with me. I'll be there for you," Norris went on.

"I don't want to go," I said quickly. "I can't, I'm sorry." I snapped the phone off and sat down on my bed. I didn't want to see Olivia's mother, in her grief, looking so much like Olivia. I knew I couldn't face it. And her friends, the ones who never came to visit her, now standing around at her funeral, talking about how much they cared. I couldn't look at those people without screaming. None of them could ever understand.

The Olivia I knew, the girl I met, was the real Olivia. The girl who died at Wilson—I didn't even know that girl. The girl with the short hair, with the scarred face. That reminder of Olivia was gone. Now all I had was my memory.

Chapter 30

My eyes are closed, but I can hear the sounds of people swimming, the bright sun warm on my face. I'm lying down, and she's next to me. When I look over at her, the sun is so bright, I can't see her face, just her profile as she sits up. She puts up one hand to shield her eyes, the wind carries her long hair back, floating. "Who are you looking for?" I ask her, as she scans the lake. "You," she says. "I'm looking for you."

———

As I brushed my teeth, I thought about the dream. It was the same, yet different every time. Sometimes I'd be sitting up on the blanket and she was beside me, her hand on my back, or she'd be walking toward me. But we were always at the lake, and I could never see her face, just a shadow of her, her silhouette, her profile, her hair blowing. I knew it was her, but she was just out of reach. No matter what I did, how I covered my eyes, the sun was hitting her just the right way so that I couldn't see her, not really. Not the way I used to.

"Mike's here," Mom called, and I threw on a T-shirt, grabbing a jacket on the way out. "Take this." Mom tried to push a toasted bagel into my hand.

"I think we're going to get something on the way," I said, but she closed my fingers around the bagel. I knew she thought I was still too skinny.

"You tell him to drive slowly, carefully." She shook her head. "I can't believe you boys talked me into this." But I could tell that part of her was thrilled that I was doing something normal—going to an outdoor concert with friends on a summer Saturday.

Mike honked and I kissed Mom on the cheek. "I'll call you, and we won't be late—the band we want to see is on this afternoon. We'll probably bail right after that." I bounced out the door and down the steps, feeling good and light. Sometimes in the morning, I would be stiff, and it could take some time for everything to click into place, but lately it had been easier, smoother. The physical therapy had paid off—my gait was pretty much normal now, no limp. Unless you asked me to touch my toes, you'd never know anything was wrong with me. "Don't take up snowboarding," the physical therapist had told me at our last session, "and you should be fine." Snowboarding and skiing were on the list of nos because of the twisting motion, something I had lost and would never get back now that my spine was fused together in two spots. A lot of things were off-limits. But there were plenty of things I could do, things I'd never tried before, like swimming, which I was really getting into.

I started going to the pool at school as therapy—taking the weight off my legs while I did some exercises. Mike joked that I was practicing for synchronized swimming, like girls do in the Olympics. "Hey, old lady, when are you getting out of that pool?" But one of the swim coaches started giving me some tips, and then I added in the practice hours. I didn't have a lot else to do. Plus I liked the feeling of being underwater. There was something about the silence of it, how the water blocked everything out, that focused me.

Now I was thinking of joining the team next year at school. The coach said I had the right build for it, and I needed to do something to fill those afternoons I used to spend at the ramps anyhow. I didn't want to even let myself get to the point where I missed biking; I wanted to fill that spot with something before it had a chance to become a hole.

"Oh come on, man, that bagel reeks like a bag of onions,"

Mike complained when I climbed in. "Eat it or get rid of it quick."

"He's nervous," Allie offered from the front seat. "You know, little miss Erin," she whispered.

"No, I'm not nervous. Just because I've been asking this girl out for six months, and she's finally going to hang out with me, why would that make me nervous? I'm sure she'll think it's very cool that I drive a ten-year-old car that smells like onions, and that I'm bringing the famous coma boy and his ex-girlfriend along for our date. I'm sure that seems totally normal to her."

I leaned up and patted his shoulder. "My mom wanted me to tell you to drive really safely, or should I remind you after you pick up Erin?"

"Now's good," Mike said. "Seriously, guys, don't mess this up for me. Just be normal."

"Oh, what will we talk about?" Allie joked. "Maybe that time Mike streaked naked through the football game last year? She might be interested in that story."

"Oh, I know," I chimed in. "I can tell her all that stuff you said about her when you visited me in the hospital. There was something about her legs, or was it her—"

"Yeah, okay, we get it," Mike interrupted. He shook his head, turning the car into the neighborhood where Erin lived. "Honestly, it never fails to freak me out when you bring up stuff that I told you when you were a vegetable."

He shook his head and turned to Allie, asking her, "I mean, doesn't that freak you out?"

Allie turned and looked back at me with a small smile. We had a long talk a couple of weeks ago about that, among other things, over coffee one afternoon. "You have this look on your face sometimes, it's like this sadness that kills me. And I just feel . . . I just hope that's not about me, or anything I did or said—or didn't say—while you were in the hospital," she explained as we sat in the café. She was right. The sadness wasn't about her, but I didn't know how to tell her what it was exactly.

"I know you've been through a lot. And I feel like I wasn't there for you as much as I could have been. But I am now." She looked down into her half-empty cup and got quiet for a moment. "I want to tell you something." She paused, looking up at me. She got so serious, I braced myself to hear something bad, like that she'd starting dating someone. But she surprised me. "You know how if you cut down a tree, you can look at the rings and see how old it is?"

I nodded.

"In bio class, our teacher was talking about how if you look closer, you can actually tell what the weather was like for each year—when the tree got lots of rain, or when there was a drought, just based on the darkness and thickness of the rings. It helps us to study the weather from hundreds of years ago, like we can look at the rings of all these trees and figure out there was a bad drought, like, fifty years ago; it's a living record."

"Okay . . . ," I said, trying to follow her.

She smiled. "Don't laugh. It made me think of you. Like, if you were a tree, how this year for you, this ring, would be light, almost invisible, a drought year. It's like a year where you almost weren't here. But you know what? There are lots more rings for you, in the future, I just know it. Lots of good rings. Solid rings. Does that make sense?"

I looked at Allie's blue eyes and her freckled face and felt nothing but love for her. She was a great girl, a true friend, even if we weren't together, even if we never were again, she was someone who cared about me, and that's all I needed to know. What had happened in the hospital, the way she handled my accident, it was forgiven. I reached over and took her hands across the table at the coffee shop and we sat like that a long time, in silence. Since then, every time I'd seen her, it was easier to hang out. I actually felt like we were closer than we'd ever been—closer than when we'd supposedly been in love.

Mike pulled up outside Erin's house. "Get in the back," he growled to Allie as Erin came out the front door. She was wearing shorts, a concert T-shirt, and a pair of cowboy boots.

"Hey," she smiled, coming over to the passenger side door. She slid in and Mike introduced us. "I've been dying to meet you! You're totally famous at school. And Mike told me we'll both be juniors next year."

Allie gave me a quick eye roll as she got settled in and Mike started the car. It wasn't long before we were at the Moonlight, a diner halfway to the city, and Mike suggested we stop. "I'm in," I said, noting that Mom had been right about the bagel. I could eat two breakfasts a day for a while and not catch up with the weight I'd managed to lose over the winter.

"So?" Mike leaned in and whispered to me as the girls walked ahead of us to get a table.

"What?" I asked. Mike motioned toward Erin, trying not to be too obvious. "Oh, she seems cool," I admitted.

"Yeah, right? She's it, I mean she is really *it*," Mike said, and I could tell he was completely gone on this girl, a full-blown crush. It was nice to see him so happy.

When we ordered and settled in, Mike seemed to relax a little bit—once it became clear that I was not going to embarrass him, and that Erin totally looked up to Allie and hung on her every word. Mike almost squirted himself with ketchup trying to get out the last drops of an empty squeeze bottle for our fries. "I'll grab a new one," I said, taking the bottle from him before he did something disastrous.

As I walked up to the counter, I heard Erin's voice behind me: "He seems so normal . . . ," and that made me smile. From what Mike and Allie had shared, I had been the talk of the school a few months ago. It was going to be a big disappointment to everyone in the fall when "coma boy" returned, looking and acting so normal—well, on the outside, at least. Maybe Mike and I should plan something special for the first day, some sort of stunt with a wheelchair or something. He'd be into that. I turned back to look at him and was relieved to see he looked more chill, his arm slung over the back of the booth.

That's when I noticed her. A girl sitting at the counter with her back to me. I felt my breath catch in my throat.

Her pale shoulders showed through the thin straps of her white sundress.

Long dark hair tumbled down her back, stopping in just the right place, above a small waist circled with a red belt.

Before I could stop myself, before I could think, I put my hand on her, touching her shoulder, her skin warm under my fingers. "Olivia," I whispered. I would know her anywhere. I wanted to breathe her in.

But the eyes that turned to me, bright and hazel, the face—no. It was wrong, all wrong.

"Hi?" the girl said curiously, looking at me.

I shook my head, trying to wake up from the dream, the vision of what I had wanted to see. "I'm sorry, I thought you were someone else."

"That's okay." The girl turned around again and left me standing there for a minute, unsure of what to do.

"Bro, ketchup!" Mike yelled, and I snapped into action, asking the server for a new bottle, which she handed me without even meeting my eyes. When I sat back down at the table, I was sweating; I could feel my forehead was wet and cold. The conversation went on around me, and I realized my friends had no idea what had just happened. Of course they didn't. Why would they? They barely remembered that day when I woke up asking for a girl named Olivia. No one remembered Olivia. No one but me.

I looked over at the girl at the counter again. Her hair was right, but the freckled arms—how could I have missed that? Of course it wasn't her. It couldn't be her. It would never be her.

As Mike shoved french fries into his mouth, making Erin giggle, I tried to pull myself back into the conversation. But my mind went to what Allie had said, about the tree and the rings inside. I realized all at once that she was wrong. The ring for this year wasn't light or barely there, it wasn't a drought. In the tree of my life, this year was a ring dark and deep, embedded further than any other year had been or ever would be. This was the year when I was hollowed out and came back from nothing. This was the year I faced everything and came out of it somehow. I wanted to think it had something to do with me, with my own strength, but I knew that wasn't true. I hadn't done it alone. I could never have done it alone.

Sometimes at night when I was at the pool, in the quiet stillness underwater, my mind would go to that place. To the hospital, to the people there. It was as if my heart could travel, over the miles, over the months that had passed, and I was back with her. Through the dark hallways, the sounds of the machines running. The feeling when I opened my eyes and she was in the room, when I had waited for her all day, and then she was there. Olivia. That closeness again. Like it used to be. But then something happens to bring me back, something in the real world. And I come back, and I'm alive; I'm me, but I'm alone. I was still getting used to that. And I wasn't sure if I was ever going to be okay with it. If I would ever stop missing her. Maybe, maybe someday. But not yet.

Allie noticed how quiet I was; she always did. "You okay?" she asked, looking at me closely.

I picked up my soda and took a sip. "Yeah." I hoped she wouldn't notice that my hand was shaking.

"Let's go!" Mike said, standing up and grabbing the check. "Good times await."

When we walked outside, I took one last look back at the girl at the counter. Through the glass from the parking lot, it could be her, if you looked at just the right angle. Almost.

I heard my name. Just a whisper.

West.

I closed my eyes and took a deep breath, let the feeling wash over me.

"You coming or what?" Mike called out. When I turned around, they were waiting for me, by the car. My friends.

"I'm coming," I said.

As I walked out of the shade and into the sun, the warmth hit my face, my shoulders. I left the darkness behind. As we pulled out of the parking lot, I didn't look back. I had what I needed, with me. Inside me. Always.

ACKNOWLEDGMENTS

This book, although fiction, required medical knowledge that was far beyond my scope. Thank you to my mom, Polly Busby, for her nursing expertise, and to my best friend, Blue Butterfield, for her medical savvy—not everything in the story is exactly medically accurate, but I got as close as possible while still protecting the story of West and Olivia.

Thank you to Karen Moy and Erik Van Rhein for sharing with me their personal story of a traumatic accident that resulted in a coma, and eventual recovery.

For his expertise and information on jail visitation, thank you to Matthew Mizel, director and producer of the documentary *On the Outs*, and volunteer with InsideOUT Writers.

Thank you to Dr. Narsing Rao and Dr. James Tan.

For sharing her true-life experience, thank you to Wendy Perez, the inspiration behind Allie's "tree of life" metaphor.

To my agent, Brenda Bowen, much gratitude for taking me on as a client and believing in me. May this be the first of many.

Thank you to Melanie Cecka, friend and editor in one, for shaping my first young-adult novel. And thanks to Victoria Wells Arms for taking this project on and seeing it safely home.

To my writers' group—Pamela Bunn, Nanci Katz Ellis, and Erin Zimring—thank you for believing in this story from the beginning.

And to my boys, Damon and August, all of my love.

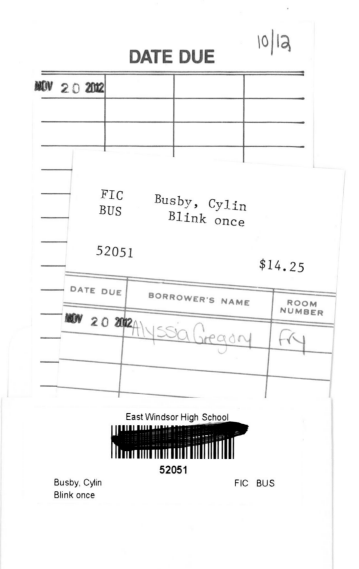